Trouble at the Manor
(Fourth Novel in the Lowenna Series)

by

Ann Summerville

Also by Ann Summerville

Storms & Secrets

The Berton Hotel

Lowenna Series

A Graceful Death

High Tide

Gwinnel Gardens

Pecan Valley Series

Grandmother's Flower Garden

Chapter 1

The blue suited scene of crime crew wasn't the first thing Gia noticed when she left her cliffside cottage in Lowenna that Friday summer morning. When she reached the bluff, she looked twice at what was once a view of the gentle ebb and flow of waves, which trickled into rock pools and rolled on to the beach. It was now covered in a foam of indiscriminate color, similar to the nicotine haze that once hung low from the ceiling of local pubs before the smoking ban.

Braving the chill morning air, Gia followed her husband, David, down the cliff road. Stopping to catch her breath, she waved him on. He was running, her pace merely a jog. Lately, they started each weekday morning with a run down the cliff road toward the beach. There they parted ways, Gia to the bench by the sea, David to run another five miles in training for an upcoming triathlon then returning home to shower before work.

At the bottom, she leaned down with her hands on her legs breathing deeply, but her eyes took in a sight she hadn't expected. Apart from a sandless beach, no flowers along the car park were visible and although it was the middle of summer, the beachfront looked like a snow storm had come in during the night and covered the car park, the buildings, and the rocks. Not the white blanket that was normally associated with the drifts of fluffy white snow, but dingy yellow trapped in the suds of the sea. But that wasn't what her eyes came to rest upon. It was the white scene of crime van and blue printed police tape stretched in a square the size of a small room. Surrounding the people wearing suits like astronauts on a moon landing, were police men and women in uniform and a detective she was familiar with. Taking her eyes from the foam covered beach, she wondered who had died.

"Miss Matthews," said Detective Inspector Barrett by way of acknowledgement.

It took her a few beats before Gia realized he'd used the wrong name.

"It's Mrs. Penrose now, but what's with the formality? You've been calling me Gia for years."

Despite the somber circumstances, he gave a weak smile, extenuating the laugh lines around his blue eyes magnified through gold rimmed glasses. He still wore his familiar tweed jacket with white cuffs protruding from the sleeves. Bits of foam had blown on the top of his graying head, looking like whipped cream on an ice cream sundae.

"Who is it?" Gia nodded toward the group of uniformed people from the police station. Without seeing beyond them, she knew from the activity that there was undoubtedly a body, prone in front of the group.

"Perhaps you could tell us," he said. "Looks like it happened last night or in the early hours. There will be little evidence left after all this mess. He turned his head toward the expanse of froth that had covered the car park, the beach and part of the sea, then took out a small notebook."

"Who found him," she paused. "Or her." The wind whipped around her and Gia pulled her shoulder length auburn hair from her face, took a band from her pocket and tied her hair in a ponytail.

"The dog."

As if to try and get their attention, a border collie with black and white markings bounded toward them.

"Oh no!" said Gia. "That's Collin Penhallow's dog, Bailey. Collin?"

Gia reached over and rested her hand on the detective's arm as if he could stop the world that was spinning out of control.

The dog sat by her feet letting out a squeaky sound, one her dogs often emitted when they wanted to go outside or to be fed. She leaned down to rub his head.

"It's not Collin," said the detective firmly, lowering his notebook.

"How do you know?" Gia stood, and straightened her back as if expecting to ward off the brunt of bad news.

"It's a woman."

"Oh."

Gia's hair quivered on the back of her neck. She shivered, then leaned down and stroked the dog again, whispering soft sounds to him. Telling him it would be all right, but both she and the dog knew it wouldn't.

"Do you want me to look?" Gia finally asked although she hoped the detective would tell her it was against procedures, wouldn't be official and she should be on her way.

Gia and the detective had experienced differences in the past, had been frustrated with each other on more than one occasion, and there had been distrust involved. But they had now come to terms with mutual respect. She still expected him to tell her to stay out of police business as he liked to put it. He bit his bottom lip and his blue eyes, magnified behind his glasses, didn't show the frown she often saw.

"Would you? Unofficial like."

"Is it bad?" asked Gia, then shook her head.

Of course it was bad. Death was never good was it?

"I wouldn't ask you if it was gruesome. She just looks like she sat in the bath for too long. She's a bit . . . discolored," he paused and studied Gia for a moment. "Discolored and wrinkled because of the foam. Looks like a head injury."

Gia nodded and the dog led her toward the body that was now enshrouded with a royal blue tarp.

The detective slightly lifted the covering and Bailey began to whine, raising his voice to a crescendo when the body was finally revealed.

The woman's face was partly covered with long matted red hair. Her face was glossy and her lips blue.

Gia simply nodded, turned away and tugged the dog behind her.

After she stepped behind the group of officers, Detective Inspector Barrett joined her.

"She must have been taking the dog for a walk. He was sitting by her," said the detective.

That struck Gia as odd as Bailey was a farm dog and ran free across the land. Why would she be taking the dog for a walk late at night or in the early hours of the morning?

"It's Meg Penhallow," Gia said. "Collin's sister."

"You're sure?"

A lump formed in her throat and Gia gulped and blinked rapidly in an effort to stave off the tears that welled in her eyes.

"I'm sure."

She didn't know Meg well, apart from being on opposing dart teams one summer. Gia hadn't gone to school in Lowenna, hadn't grown up there and had only spent summers in the seaside village with her aunt Grace. Many of the locals weren't well known to her. But Gia knew someone who would know all about both Meg and her brother and she intended to stop by the King William pub at opening time where Holly worked. Her friend knew more about the town than the annual census.

Gia returned to her cottage perched upon the cliff with its white washed walls, robin egg blue trim and white fence. The house had once belonged to her Aunt Grace, her dad's sister, and she spent many hours there during the summer months when she had longed to get out of the city, away from the constant snake of traffic with its exhaust fume smells and most of all away from her mother. Aunt Grace had given her a quiet respite. That was until she had died an untimely death two years ago.

After feeding her dogs and taking a quick shower, Gia grabbed her notebook and laptop and opened the door.

"Off to the shop, then?" shouted Rose Lanner from her house on the other side of the driveway.

Rose was both Gia's neighbor and mother-in-law and her appearance hadn't changed in years. She still wore an apron over her dress, both of which were covered in flowers of different colors and hues. Her hair was short and peppered with gray and it looked as if she'd been in a wind storm even when there was barely a breeze.

Gia nodded, deciding to wait until later to tell Rose about the death in the depths of the foam, not far from where Lowenna Antiques, that they were part owners in, was located.

"David's still running," Gia said.

"He's taking this tri . . . tri . . ." Rose stuttered.

"Triathlon."

"Yes. That's it," said Rose. "He's taking it seriously."

David, her husband, took everything seriously. Whether it was inserting a screw, organizing someone's accounting system or simply drying a plate, he did it methodically and thoroughly.

"No other news, then?" asked Rose while staring at Gia's mid-section. "Been married seven months now."

Gia had heard that stress often caused women to have trouble conceiving and each time she left her house and saw Rose staring at her was enough stress to cause her whole body to seize. Not that Rose said anything unkindly. Gia knew the woman who had first been Aunt Grace's neighbor, then Gia's friend and finally her mother-in-law was anxious to have grandchildren.

5

David had said it would happen in good time, and not to worry. But she did worry. Rose was right. It had been seven months.

But Gia didn't voice her concerns. She simply said "See you later."

"I'll be down dreckley," said Rose.

Gia watched Rose turn toward the sea, but before they could discuss the state of the waterfront, she had started her car and headed back down the cliff path.

She passed the fishermen's cottages, that had stood for a century or more, their inhabitants had watched for a father or husband out fishing for pilchards or herring. They were now mostly bed and breakfast establishments taking advantage of the onslaught of holidaymakers from London and the Midlands during the summer, heading like a procession from the cities. Locals called them emmets. Cornish for ants.

The village of Lowenna was nestled between two hills and facing the sea. A harbor wall of large dark gray stones, which had stood for more than a hundred years, lunged out into the water leaving behind a sheltered inlet for fishing boats and charter boats for summer tourists. Not far from the harbor was Lowenna Antiques, a shop that Gia, Rose and their friend Susan had purchased when Gia first moved to the village. At the bottom of the hill was a park where Gia had played as a child and a village pub, The King William IV, sat behind a pond often used as a boating lake for miniature craft. An arbor from the park led to St. Bartholomew's Church abutting the green.

She reached the car park and the crowd had grown. Tourists, having eaten their breakfast of eggs, bacon, baked beans, sausage and tomatoes followed by toast and marmalade, had waddled down to take in the scene.

She waved to David, who had completed his circuit and was running, a little slower, up the hill. She still got butterflies, fluttering in her tummy, when she saw him, felt her palms moisten and at times she even blushed. In his early thirties, David was dark complected with boyish good looks. He had brown eyes and a smile that melted her heart. They'd been childhood friends which developed into a romance when Aunt Grace had left Gia the cottage and she'd returned to Lowenna to make her home there.

Tomorrow David would train on his bicycle and the following day . . . Gia wondered if the foam would be gone and if there would be any ill effects. Perhaps she would suggest that he put off the swimming part of his training for a few days.

"The froth," said Susan Brea when both she and Rose Lanner joined Gia in Lowenna Antiques which the three of them owned.

"That mess outside?" asked Rose.

"Yes. It's sea foam," Susan continued.

Susan, although the oldest, was the smaller of the trio, reaching a height of just over five feet. Her hair that, apart from when she was singing in a talent show at the local hall, had never been out of the bun on the top of her head, was a mousy brown color with a few wayward white strands. She had tiny features, but tended to wear bulky shoes and clothes.

"Don't look like any foam I've ever seen," said Rose.

Gia was thankful that whatever it was in those suds, hadn't reached the door of their shop and the pavement was relatively clear.

"Like The Blog," said Susan. "Although that wasn't from the sea."

"Whose blog," Gia wanted to know.

"That film with Steve McQueen in it. It covered everything. Just ate it all up and every time it ate something it got bigger," said Susan. "He was a lovely man. Did all his own stunts and everything."

"She means the film, The Blob," clarified Rose. "It was in the late 50s. Before your time, Gia. And I very much doubt whatever that mess is on the beach that it came from outer space."

"You're right," said Susan.

Rose stood straighter and puffed out her ample chest.

"It didn't come from outer space," said Susan. "What happened was . . ." said their friend who had become adept at using Google ". . . high winds whipped up the sea spray from the incoming tide into froth. Like in a washing machine."

"You'd have to have Tide to make the suds in a washing machine."

Both Gia and Susan paused to see if Rose had said this as a joke.

She hadn't. But regardless, Susan couldn't help but take advantage of the slip.

"Of course," Susan said. "Persil or Gain wouldn't have the same effect." She smiled and her thin lips widened.

"What are you talking about?" asked Rose. "You know I always use Tide."

"Do you think it was just the wind?" asked Gia.

"Not only the wind," continued Susan. She paused as if trying to picture her computer screen that morning. "Organic material. Organic material in the sea's eco system."

Rose suddenly laughed a low belly laugh and rather than join in, both Susan and Gia turned toward her wondering which one of them was the brunt of her joke.

"Funny if it was Tide though," said Rose. "Tide washing powder."

Both women stared at her.

"Get it? Tide. Sea."

They all laughed.

A lone police car stopped by the edge of the car park and all three women turned toward the window.

"What's he doing here?" asked Rose.

"Scene of crime people were there first thing this morning," said Gia.

"By the beach?" asked Susan. "Why?"

"I talked to Detective Inspector Barrett. It was Meg Penhallow."

"Missing?" asked Rose.

"Dead," said Susan.

Gia nodded.

"Must have been a blunt instrument," offered Susan.

"What?" asked Rose.

"It's always a blunt instrument," said Susan. "That is . . . unless it's a stabbing, then obviously it isn't blunt."

"Meg is about your age isn't she?" asked Rose. "I mean was."

And Meg had been. It was too young to die, too young to be the victim of a crime - a murder. Rose was fond of rhetorical questions and Gia didn't respond.

All three of them bowed their heads as if in silent prayer.

"Where was her brother? Those two are, were, always together," said Rose.

"I don't know, but their dog, Bailey was with her. The detective was going to take him up to the farm and let Collin know what had happened."

"I wonder if he's the prime suspect?" asked Susan who watched too many mystery programs on television.

Before the three of them could discuss further the intricacies of the British Broadcasting Corporation mysteries, the bell of the shop tinkled and Ruth Rundle maneuvered her walker into the shop.

Gia pulled out a chair for her by the table that the three owners of Lowenna Antiques had their afternoon tea on and sometimes morning coffee.

"Take a load off," said Rose and raised her eyebrows toward Susan.

Gia had long given up trying to decipher the codes between the two ladies.

"Coffee," said Susan. "I'll put the kettle on."

"We're just about to have our morning coffee, Madam Mayor," said Rose.

Quite expecting her to bow or worse still, curtsey, Gia excused herself and went into the tiny kitchen to help Susan retrieve the biscuit tin that was always full.

"Embarrassing, that's what it is," said Susan as she lined up four Willow Pattern cups and saucers. "The woman was mayor once, I'll give her that, but it's not as if she's royalty and she wasn't even mayor of Lowenna."

"You know Rose," said Gia which provoked a sigh from both of them.

Yes, they knew Rose and although she professed to dislike having to pay for the royal family, Rose did like a bit of pomp and circumstance and tended to insert it even at times when it wasn't warranted.

"Just call me, Ruth," said the former mayor when Gia put the biscuit tin on the table.

She wondered if Rose had called the woman your worshipfulness which is a word she used for people of dignitary status.

"Susan!" Rose shouted. "Plate."

Of course, Rose wouldn't want their old biscuit tin to be centered on the table. Biscuits should be arranged neatly on a plate.

"I'll get it," Gia offered.

The former mayor seemed to glow with the attention from Rose or it could have been the effect of too much powdered blush. She was a small rotund lady, with red hair which had a brassy tint. She occasionally lifted the eye glasses with a multi colored frame that hung from an equally multi colored beaded necklace and peered at the table.

"Gia's been married for seven months now," said Rose and all three women stared at Gia who gripped her hands in front of her.

"Nice," said Ruth with a tone that showed she didn't think it nice at all. "Some women like children. Myself, I've never been much for them."

"But weren't you—" Susan was cut off abruptly by Rose who gave her a glaring look.

Ruth stared at the Willow Pattern on her cup as if the picture would conjure up the answer she was looking for.

"Of course," said Ruth. "I was married once. The poor man died suddenly and that was the end of that."

She spoke as if she'd just discovered that she'd inadvertently missed the expiration date on a can of tuna.

"Poor man," agreed Rose.

"Speaking of deaths," Susan continued and turned her back to Rose. "Do you know anything about Meg Penhallow?"

Ruth studied her cup again before raising it to her lips, returning it to the saucer and carefully spooning in two heaps of sugar.

"Penahallow?" Ruth asked.

"The woman who died this morning," offered Gia. "She was found underneath all that foam in the car park."

"Never mind all that now. What can we do for you, Mrs. Rundle?" asked Rose.

Susan quickly held the plate of biscuits toward the former mayor. "Have a custard cream," she offered.

"I was looking for replacement dishes. Spode," said Ruth taking two biscuits. "I broke a plate and saucer. It had a picture of an English Springer Spaniel on them."

"Woodland Hunting Dogs," said Gia. "It's part of the Woodland Hunting Dogs collection. You must be a dog lover,"

Gia felt the need to bond with anyone who loved dogs as much as she.

"Can't abide them," said Ruth. "I broke a plate and saucer when I was up at the manor, stupid dog jumped up at me and I dropped the lot. The cup survived though. You'd think pedigrees would be better behaved."

"Susan. Look and see if we have any," said Rose.

"We don't," Gia responded a little more abruptly than she had intended.

Whether it was because she didn't want to sell anything to someone who didn't love dogs, or if she could recollect that there weren't any in their inventory, she wasn't sure. But then she thought about Mrs. Gillard at the manor. She loved dogs and would probably have been broken hearted that the plate and saucer were destroyed.

"We can probably order you one," said Gia without much enthusiasm.

"That's it, Mayor Ruth," said Rose. "We'll order them for you."

"Wonderful," said the ex-mayor, selecting a biscuit and taking a bite, then pocketing three more.

Gia stood by the door and watched Ruth Rundle walk slowly toward her Skoda estate car. Something wasn't quite right about the way Ruth was walking. She was pushing the walker but didn't seem to be leaning on it or using it to balance herself.

"What was that all about?" asked Susan when the bell tinkled yet again and Gia closed the door. "I'm sure I've seen some of those plates in the back."

Gia shrugged. "I'll look in a minute. What's wrong with her?"

"All sorts of things," said Rose. "Fibromyalgia, lumbar spondy something or other, frozen shoulder, arthritis, back problems."

"Thank goodness for the disability living allowance. That's what's kept her going," said Susan. She's only in her fifties."

"Late fifties," added Rose. "She's in her late fifties - nearly sixty."

Apparently there was a big difference between fifties and sixties of which Susan and Rose was the latter.

Whatever illness or illnesses Ruth Rundle was experiencing, they certainly didn't seem as disabling as everyone thought. Gia watched her, through the window, toss the walker in the boot of her car and climb behind the wheel and with a quick glance in her rearview mirror, she eased on to the street and drove off.

Chapter 2

"So, where's David tonight?" asked Holly when Gia slid on to a bar stool at the King William pub later that evening.

"Working."

"I thought he was supposed to be in training," said Holly.

"He is. David ran this morning," Gia slid a few pound coins on to the bar. "Wine spritzer, please."

"Not by the promenade where that body was found?" asked Holly, taking out a glass from under the bar. "A few of the coppers came in at lunch time. They said it was quite a mess what with all that frothy stuff."

"I saw D.I. Barrett. He asked me to identify her."

"I heard it was Meg Penhallow," said Holly.

"It was." Gia's shoulders slumped. "Oh! Holly. She looked terrible. Remember how pretty her long red hair used to be? All those soft waves. It was covered in that foam stuff."

"Do you know how she died?" asked Holly. "Perhaps she slipped on the rocks," she offered.

Holly poured white wine into the glass, added club soda and handed the drink to Gia.

"I don't know. It looked like she was taking Bailey for a walk because he was sitting with her when the police showed up."

"I wonder who called it in."

Now there's a point, thought Gia. Who had called it in? Did they dial nine-nine-nine or simply call the Lowenna police?

"The police must think it's suspicious, otherwise why would scene of crime people be there?" asked Gia.

"I think they do that automatically these days, but I don't know. Her brother will be broken hearted. Collin was really close to her. I think he was a year younger. Meg was supposed to be getting married in the spring. Speaking of marriage," said Holly. "How's everything going? I don't see much of you these days."

"It's good," Gia couldn't think of anything to expound upon.

It *was* good. Both she and David had drifted into a routine. They'd known each other long enough to be comfortable. But there was that one thing that just kept tugging at Gia, like an annoying brother, tap-tap-tapping at her mind.

"No sign yet?" asked Holly.

And there it was. Another person to question Gia's fertility – her ability to carry on the Penrose name.

Holly hadn't seemed to expect an answer and turned to pull pump handles, tilting the pint glass just enough to fill it with amber liquid and very little froth or head as the locals liked to call it. Holly was a good barmaid. She took care of the patrons, listened to their problems, gave them empathy when needed and on top of that she was good to look at.

Holly wasn't the height of style, but she always seemed as if she'd spent hours in front of the mirror. In fact, Holly did very little to look as good as she did.

Holly drummed her long bronze finger nails on the bar. The wood varnish was chipped and pock marked from years of use. Her dark brown hair, that had once reached her waist, was cut shoulder length, giving it more body and bounce. She wore a top with purple embellishments and the word *Italia* written across the chest, edged with tiny diamond-like studs.

After passing the glass of ale to a patron, Holly turned to Gia.

"So?"

It hadn't been a rhetorical question as she had hoped.

"No sign," responded Gia with a sigh that came from deep within.

"It will happen," said Holly.

But how did she know? How did anyone know? They had talked about children long before they became married, or even engaged.

"David wants children?" she said and was surprised that she'd said it out loud.

"And you don't?" Holly took a step back and lowered the cloth she was using to wipe the bar.

"Of course I do. Oh, Holly, what if we can't have kids. What if it's my fault?"

"Have you talked to your doctor?"

"I'm scared to."

"Give it some time. Enjoy being married for a while. It's only been seven months and you're no spring chicken."

"I'm thirty-two!"

"Not a teenager. They seem to get pregnant at the drop of a hat."

Gia looked around the room and Holly left to serve another customer. It never occurred to her that she wouldn't get pregnant right away. They'd joked about it on their honeymoon while they sat on the balcony of their cruise ship. They'd planned on a September baby.

"Did you even find out if your marriage is legal?" asked Holly when she returned.

That was another thing they had laughed about while sipping wine on the balcony and watching the azure Caribbean sea swirl away from the ship. After the wedding party and guests had been cut off by a snow storm on the evening of the wedding, Susan announced she was an ordained minister. What she hadn't told them was that she had found a web site and paid twenty pounds to receive the ordination allowing her to perform weddings. Unfortunately it was for weddings in the state of Texas.

"The captain married us. Apparently getting married is acceptable as long as the ship is registered in a country where marriage at sea is legal. Ironically, if it's a ship registered in the United Kingdom then it wouldn't be."

"That doesn't make sense."

"Our laws state that it has to be somewhere that the public has access to in case someone wants to object to the wedding and a cruise ship isn't somewhere public."

"Who makes this stuff up?" asked Holly.

"Someone who has nothing better to do than make people's lives complicated I would guess."

Holly stepped away again and Gia watched her in the mirror behind the bar. Holly had the most amazing almond shaped eyes that looked beautiful even without makeup. Her dark hair had a slight wave and she always wore big ear-rings that looked glamorous on her, but on Gia they looked no different from hanging gaudy Christmas decorations on her ears. She looked again at the mirror, this time at her own reflection. Her auburn hair that was chin length, had far too many waves and was often frizzy with the damp weather. Her nose was small with a smattering of freckles. She had hazel eyes that she thought seemed too small even with the most artistic efforts at putting on eye makeup.

Holly placed a basket with French bread, a large slice of Cheddar cheese and a pickled onion in front of Gia.

"Someone ordered it and changed their mind. I know it's your favorite."

Gia hadn't felt hungry, hadn't felt like eating after the upset of that morning, but suddenly her tummy growled. She'd skipped breakfast and the sandwich at lunch time hadn't done much to fill her up.

"Thanks."

Holly was right. Ploughman's lunch was her favorite.

She buttered the bread and placed the cheese in between the two halves of a six inch piece of French bread, then bit into the pickled onion.

Gia paused and glanced around the pub that had been a go to place for her when she had lived alone and needed company. Even the stale air was somewhat comforting and familiar.

The walls were painted white. The uneven plaster left patterned shadows on the wall which were criss-crossed with dark wooden beams. The same dark wood was on the ceiling, each beam parallel to the other. Between were circular recessed lights. Gold swirled on the forest green carpet, not as bright as it had once been. There was a door leading to the pond, which locals called a boating lake, and another door opposite leading to the outside patio where trestle tables were lined up in the walled courtyard.

"Here comes P.C. Plod," said Gia when the door opened. "He might be able to tell us something about Meg," she suggested.

"Trouble is you never know what tale he's spinning to make himself look good." Holly pulled down a pewter tankard from the row of hooks holding beer mugs for locals. Each had an engraved name on the base.

Gia considered this. Holly was right. P.C. Jones couldn't be trusted, but at least there might be some truth in what he said. She stared at the mullioned window through which filtered light shone weakly through. The sun had begun its descent toward the horizon.

"Usual, P.C. Jones?" Holly asked.

"Just a half. I'm on duty," he said and pulled out a stool next to Gia.

Gia jumped right in with her questions. "Any news about Meg Penhallow?" she asked.

"News travels fast."

"Gia was there," said Holly pushing the tankard toward P.C. Jones and sliding the coins from the bar into her palm.

"You were?" He took out a black notebook, flipped over a page, licked the end of his pencil and began writing. "What time?"

"I don't know. Ask Detective Inspector Barrett. He was there too," said Gia. "I didn't discover the body if that's what you're asking."

He returned the notebook to the top pocket of his dark blue uniform.

"Was it an accident?" Holly asked.

"We won't know until the medical examiner takes a look. Had a nasty gash on her head, she did."

"So it was murder?" asked Holly.

"She could have slipped on the rocks. With all that foam and mess along the beach, she wouldn't have been able to see where she was going especially if it happened Thursday night."

"But she was in the car park," observed Gia. "There weren't any rocks there."

"Rubbish bins had been blown over in the storm. She could have tripped on one of them," offered the policeman.

That would be possible, but it had to be something sharp and she couldn't think of anything that might be sticking up that Meg may have fallen on.

The policeman downed his beer and took his hat from the bar. "Off to Truro to take a test Monday," he said with an importance that neither of the girls acknowledged.

He paused as if waiting for a response and when none came, he left.

"What was that all about?" asked Gia.

"He wants to be a detective," said Holly. "He's always taking tests to try and get a promotion, but they usually don't come to anything. Is his wife still in the knitting circle?"

Gia nodded. Mrs. Jones *was* in the knitting circle and drove them all crazy. Both her and her husband didn't think anyone who wasn't born in the area was of much importance. They hated all the changes to Cornwall, with people buying holiday homes and many commuters taking advantage of the faster trains to work in the city during the week and come home to a house in Cornwall at the week-end.

19

"She's still a pain in the arse, I assume," Holly snickered. Then her expression changed abruptly. "Should we go and see Collin?"

"Perhaps give it a day or two and head up there. I'll ask Rose if she could make him a shepherd's pie, she does a better job than I do."

"I'll ask mum to make him a cake," said Holly.

Both girls made eye contact and laughed.

"I guess neither of us did well in home economics," said Holly.

Gia, for the second time that day, walked up the cliff road. Winds had mostly dissipated. The foam that had once covered the car park, public toilets, and the bridge that crossed the river heading out to sea, was sparse.

It was still light when she reached the cottage that stood on the cliffs with a view of the beach and sea and had once belonged to her aunt. Aunt Grace's sudden death had been a blow to Gia and she had felt lost when she first arrived in Lowenna. That was until she realized that the villagers from Lowenna were welcoming her. Especially Rose who had been Aunt Grace's neighbor. After two years, she now considered Lowenna her home and the cottage had been a haven for her, but not so much now.

There was a chill in the air when Gia reached the cottage. She sent the dogs outside and turned on the shower relishing in the hot spray on her back and shoulders.

Feeling more relaxed, she let the dogs in, checked the answer phone for messages – none from David. In fact none from anyone. She was afraid this would happen and it had. Married life had cut her off. No one called in the evenings. No one invited her anywhere and the only questions she was asked these days was when they could expect a little Penrose to be born.

Not for the first time, she wondered if she and David would have fared better if they had stayed engaged and not taken that final step. But no, she wouldn't want to go back to how things were. She loved waking up next to David in the morning, loved feeling his arms around her when she went to sleep at night and loved how he did little things to please her. Little things like putting the toothpaste on her brush in the morning. Hanging up her robe when she left it on the floor in the bathroom and cooking them dinner.

"We don't want any more fires," he had once said.

But that was unfair because there hadn't been an actual fire. Simply a blocked chimney and it had caused a lot of smoke and had nothing to do with the dinner she was cooking. She doubted she would ever live that one down.

She checked her mobile phone which let out a beep. A text message from David said he would be home late. She sent a text message back to him. When had that happened? When had they started sending text messages instead of speaking to each other on the phone?

Canute and Daisy lay at her feet, the only two constants in her pre and post-marriage life. Canute's black and merle coat glistened in the waning light. She had found him on the beach when she first moved to Lowenna and he had settled in, as if he had always known this would be his home. Daisy had been with her in London and now loved having a garden instead of a city flat. Gia rubbed her hand through the wiry hair of the terrier-mix dog. She pulled a long strand of grass from the sandy colored hair. Canute snored softly with his head buried between his two oversized paws.

Gia left the sleeping dogs, and filled an electric kettle with water. Even the kettle had been unfamiliar. David had brought it with him from his flat and she missed the whistle of her stainless steel one that she used to put on the stove.

Filling her favorite mug, the one with painted pansies that had once been Aunt Grace's and therefore comforting, Gia swirled an Earl Gray tea bag in the hot water, relishing the perfumed aroma from the bag.

She propped pillows up on her bed, swapping hers with David's with its familiar scent. She savored the hot tea and opened her diary.

It was there that David found her a few hours later, slumped amongst the pillows with the diary resting on her chest and a half filled cup of tea beside the bed.

Chapter 3

Gia awoke with a start, noticing her jeans on the floor and beside her an empty space.

"David!"

He appeared at the bedroom door and placed a hot cup of coffee on the bedside table.

"What time did you get home?" Gia asked.

"It was late, but the good news is that I won't have to go in today. I haven't had a Saturday morning off in ages. You were out like a light when I got home," he said, standing by the window. "I didn't want to disturb you, but you looked so uncomfortable." He opened the blinds and Gia blinked against the sunlight.

She could imagine David coming home, not to a loving wife, but a snoring lump in the bed. Only David would think to pull off her jeans so that she would be more comfortable and pull the blanket over her. She looked over at her diary and wondered if he had simply closed it or taken a look. Writing down her most intimate thoughts had started when she was in her preteens and a habit she had never broken.

"Come back to bed," she said, patting the spot next to her that was still warm.

"Can't. I'm making us breakfast and then I'm off to train."

Gia took in his shirt with the Adidas logo, his bike shorts and blue and luminous green running shoes. He'd shaved his legs which he said improved his speed.

His face showed a sympathetic frown. "I'm sorry. Look we'll do something this afternoon."

"I need to work in the antique shop this afternoon."

This was all her own fault. She'd wanted David to take up a hobby, wanted him to make friends and wanted to have some time for herself. She had worried that the two of them would be under each other's feet and lose the spark that was between them. But David was obsessive with anything he did and while she had been pleased at their wedding when he announced he would be training for a triathlon, she now found that it kept the two of them apart far more than she would have liked.

Gia moved her legs over the side of the bed, but David leaned over and pushed her back toward the pillows. He kissed her, then gently lifted her legs on to the bed. She smiled. He'd changed his mind and they could snuggle in bed for a while, and maybe . . .

"You stay there," he said. "I'll have your breakfast out in a jiffy. Breakfast in bed for my princess."

How could she argue with that? He tried so hard to make her happy.

"You're the best," she said and she meant it. "Perhaps tomorrow we can have a lie in."

David bit his lip.

"Training tomorrow too?" she said and her heart plunged.

"I'll go later. If the foam has cleared, I'll swim. It will be warmer in the afternoon."

Not by much. The Atlantic was cold at the best of times, but David had bought a wet suit and he wouldn't be coming out of the water with a blue tinge like she did on the rare occasions when she went in the sea, making sure to never let the water cover more than her waist.

"Don't forget we've invited my parents and yours for Sunday dinner tomorrow," she said as he retreated. "At noon," she added, but doubted he had heard her.

The back door opened and she wondered if he was leaving, but the tinkle of dog tags told her he was letting the dogs outside. They returned a few minutes later and she heard the metal tags pinging against their dog bowls followed by loud lapping from the water bowl.

When he brought in a meal worthy of any local bed and breakfast establishment, he placed the tray on her lap, and sat on the bed.

"You heard about Meg Penhallow?" he asked.

"I stopped and talked to Detective Inspector Barrett," she said. "Meg was found in the car park."

"I saw John there, but didn't want to stop. I know the police hate it when a crowd forms while they're trying to do their job."

David and John Barrett occasionally got together for a drink. It was David who introduced D.I. Barrett to Gia after her aunt died.

"Are they sure it was her?" he asked.

"I identified her. The detective asked if I would see if it was anyone I knew. There was no identification on her."

"Collin is going to be broken up. He was upset enough that she was getting married, but this . . ."

He let the thought trail off.

"Broken up enough to stop her?" asked Gia.

Unlike Gia, David had grown up in Lowenna, gone to school there and knew most of the locals.

With her knife, she pushed baked beans on to her fork, but half of them fell before reaching her mouth and landed on her t-shirt. She scooped them up and placed them on the side of her plate.

"By killing her? That doesn't make any sense," said David.

"It could have been an accident, but some say that their relationship was unnatural for a brother and sister."

"You know how gossips are. I'm surprised you would listen to that nonsense," David's voice was clipped with a tone of agitation.

And he was right. She shouldn't listen.

"And . . ." David paused until she made eye contact with him. "I know how much you like a mystery," he turned to look at the stack of books, mostly mysteries, towered on the bedside table. ". . . but this isn't a game. Stay out of it, Gia."

"Are you forbidding me to get involved?" she laughed.

He shook his head. David knew her well enough and regardless of his pleas she would be right there annoying Detective Inspector Barrett at every turn.

"I know better," he said. "Eat your eggs before they get cold. How about I take you out to dinner tonight? That little restaurant in Truro. The one in the old chapel?"

"Two meals in one day, Mr. Penrose. I could quite get used to this."

"You're on your own for lunch," he said and with a kiss on her cheek, he was out the door and she imagined him cycling down the hill.

Only a few scattered blobs of foam remained when she hooked on Daisy and Canute's leashes. Rose opened her side door, shook out a mat and waved across the driveway. Their houses were identical in size, but the room layout reversed, and Gia imagined how sad it had been for Rose when Aunt Grace had died. Both widowed, they had shared a bond. But Rose had remarried and behind her neighbor Gia saw the balding head of Paul Lanner, a sweet, rotund man who had given up a garage flat and moved in with Rose after their marriage.

"Going to the shop later?" asked Rose.

Gia nodded. "After lunch."

Not that she would want any lunch after eating bacon, eggs, baked beans, tomatoes along with toast and blackberry jam. The problem was, if it was in front of her, Gia felt compelled to eat it.

"Come before lunch," shouted Rose. "Susan's making sandwiches and a cake."

Gia's stomach felt like the rush of the incoming tide and she gulped back a wave of nausea.

"Okay," she said with more enthusiasm than she felt.

26

Rose closed the door and Gia took a moment to breath in the brisk sea air, inhaling the briny smell. Canute tugged at his leash and the trio headed down the hill and past the car park. She glanced at the spot where the policemen had been huddled the day before. There was something bothering her about the scene yesterday, but she couldn't put her finger on it.

"Nice day," said Mrs. Trewellyn when Gia reached the shop that Iris Trewellyn and her husband ran when he wasn't out on his fishing boat.

Iris Trewellyn had been a long time friend of the three ladies who ran Lowenna Antiques. She was a tall, slim lady with straight snowy hair cut into a bob, framing her face and falling just below her ear lobes. She was dressed in a straight striped cotton skirt of primary colors and a white blouse. Around her neck a cross dangled from a gold chain.

"Did Mr. Trewellyn go out on his boat?" asked Gia.

"Left with the tide," she said, her voice soft with a West Country lilt. "I'll stop by later. What time are you opening?"

"Susan should be there now."

"Is David coming later to do the shopping?" Iris asked.

"He's out training."

It was then that Gia realized David had taken over most of the household chores. She did very little at the house and always accepted when he offered to pick up groceries on his way home. She vowed to try harder and help out, but David was the one who was particular about the house, just as her Aunt Grace had been. Gia didn't care much if clothes were on the floor, if the toothpaste had a cap or there were dishes in the sink. But he also cared about the things that were important to her. She should do the same for him.

She walked the two dogs down the street, past the green grocers, past the estate agents and past a shop selling souvenir trinkets and t-shirts. It was at the butcher's shop that she stopped and stared at red meat arranged in the refrigerated window.

Blood.

Meg Penhallow.

Even with the foam covering much of Meg's body, shouldn't it have been tinged with red.

Shouldn't there have been a lot of blood?

Why wasn't there a pool of red beneath Meg's head?

Still frowning and thoughts swirling through her mind, she absently waved to David as he passed her on his bicycle, nodded to Susan who was standing outside Lowenna Antiques and barely acknowledged Paul as he passed in his van.

She would need to talk to Detective Inspector Barrett. No matter how much David didn't want her to be involved she had already solved three murders in Lowenna. While wondering what the crime statistics had been before she moved here, she considered a murder once a year far too many for such a small village.

"About time you got here," said Susan after Gia had taken the two dogs home and returned to Lowenna Antiques. "What was the matter with you when you stood outside the butcher's shop? You looked like you'd seen a ghost." Susan paused and her eyes twinkled as if a burst of power had ignited them. "Not feeling queasy looking at the meat were you?"

Gia shook her head so fast that she immediately got a headache not unlike when she ate ice cream too fast.

"No. I just had a thought."

Susan turned her head to the side so far that her ear nearly rested on her shoulder and her bun bobbed on top of her head. This was her silent way of asking a question.

"Meg Penhallow," said Gia. "There wasn't any blood. If she had a blow to the head wouldn't there be a lot of blood."

"Why don't you boogle it," said Susan who liked to think she was up on the latest internet lingo, but invariable got it wrong. "My laptop is in the kitchen."

She said *laptop* almost proudly as if it were a winning medal. Gia wondered why it was in the tiny kitchenette that had little more than a small fridge, a sink, a microwave oven and a few shelves for cups and plates.

"I couldn't live without boogle these days," continued Susan.

"It's . . ." Gia stopped and decided not to correct her friend. Rose so often burst Susan's bubble. She didn't want to do the same.

"You can unplug the camera, it's probably charged by now."

That explained why it was in the kitchen, but what had Susan been doing? There was no telling.

Gia didn't unplug the laptop because it wasn't plugged into the outlet. Although a USB cable connected a camera.

"Did you say you want the camera unplugged?" Gia shouted.

"Yes. It should be charged. I left it overnight."

"To transfer pictures?" Gia asked.

"No, silly, to charge the battery, but it doesn't seem to be working."

Gia disconnected the camera from the USB port and slid open the door to the camera compartment that held batteries.

"You need two of these," said Gia and handed Susan the batteries from the camera. "This . . ." she held up the cable. ". . . is to transfer pictures."

"But I don't have any pictures, yet?" said Susan, obviously confused.

Deciding no good could come of continuing this conversation, Gia gave Susan a quick hug and connected to the internet. Susan returned to the shop and Gia could hear her rummaging in the catch all box behind the counter. Probably looking for batteries.

Beside Gia were a pile of sandwiches, a bowl of Twiglets, and a chocolate cake along with a glass holding celery stalks.

"Blunt instrument," shouted Susan. "Look up what happens when someone is hit with a blunt instrument."

"It says here . . ." but Gia stopped. Should she be telling Susan what she had found? It was gruesome.

But Susan had come in and was on tip toe leaning over Gia's shoulder.

"Bone fragments pounded into the brain," read Susan. "There, it says the assailant would be covered in blood. What you have to do is look for someone covered in blood and wulla."

Gia turned to Susan who had her hands on her hips and was smiling proudly like a child that had taken its first steps.

"Wulla?" repeated Gia.

"I'm learning French. It means *there it is*," said Susan.

Gia was pretty sure the word was voila, but at least Susan was using it in the correct instance. She was just grateful that she'd given up trying to speak in Cornish.

"Is that making you feel sick, looking at those bloody pictures?" asked Susan who didn't wait for a reply. "Of course," Susan, satisfied that she'd solved one problem and could go on to sharing her latest endeavor. "If you were feeling a bit sick, tummy upset that is, mal de mer," she added, using the French term. "I could give you some of my Kwells."

"No, I'm fine. But why are you taking tablets for sea-sickness. You hate the water."

The two of them moved from the kitchen into the shop and Gia straightened a plate on the shelf, making a mental note to get out the duster later.

"I read this book and it said you should just jump in and take care of whatever fears you have," said Susan. "It would make life easier."

Gia couldn't argue with that. She had a fear of water, the sea in particular, and had once swum out farther than she would have liked to rescue her dog. Not that she could consider it overcoming a fear, because she still didn't like to go out farther than where she could touch the bottom.

"Jump in is probably not the best way to look at it," said Gia with a smile.

"I'll be on a boat. No jumping involved. Look at this." Susan held up a brochure.

"Shark fishing!" said Rose who had come in the shop. "You're going shark fishing? Have you lost your mind, Susan?"

"Whenever I do, it comes back eventually," said Susan laughing at her own joke.

Gia had to agree with Rose. Shark fishing for someone who was as petite as Susan didn't seem like a good idea.

"Wouldn't it pull you over the boat?" she asked.

"No worries. She won't catch anything," said Rose. "Is that why you've been taking all that stuff?"

Susan pocketed the packet of Kwells.

"I think you only have to take it an hour before you leave," said Gia.

"I'm going this afternoon. Got my ticket," Susan pulled a ticket for the charter boat from an apron pocket that was bulging and looked like a hamster's cheek.

Gia groaned and Rose made the sign of the cross even though she wasn't Catholic.

"This wouldn't have anything to do with Percy Legg would it?" asked Rose.

"Maybe."

"Who's Percy Legg?" asked Gia.

"He owns the Mermaid," said Rose.

"He says mermaids show him where the sharks are," said Susan.

"How would you be able to reel it in?" Gia wanted to know.

"His son is the one who charters the boat. He's a big man. Lots of muscles." Susan did a strong man pose. "You can come and see me off if you like."

"Well, as you're leaving the two of us to run the shop," said Rose. "I don't see that happening."

Gia looked at Susan whose chin was coming dangerously close to touching her chest. She knew from past experience that once her chin and chest made contact, her eyes would well with tears.

"Surely, we can shut up shop for a little while," Gia offered. "But it looks like you made us a lovely lunch. Let's tuck in shall we?"

At that, Susan's chin shot up and she smiled.

"Lunch will be served dreckley," she said and her trainers squeaked as she hopped into the kitchen.

It was an hour later that the three ladies walked across the street to the harbor. Boats were tied along the quay and red, yellow and green water craft bobbed with the tide. It was easy to spot the Mermaid because ladies of the sea had been painted along the side.

Susan waved frantically and shouted "Bonjour," which the wind whipped away across the ocean toward a land where they might just understand what Susan was shouting.

They followed her along the old harbor stones until the three of them reached the boat.

Percy spread out his arms and hugged Susan so tightly that he lifted her off the ground.

He had once been a tall man, but now had a slight stoop. Percy looked the part - a weathered fisherman. He wore a blue knitted hat, blue long sleeved t-shirt. His blue trousers were held up by a blue silver buckled belt. His lips were thin and if he had teeth, Gia couldn't see any. His jowls were shaped with what looked like a parenthesis outlining his mouth and a bulbous nose. But it was his eyes that Gia noticed. Although sunken, there was a kindliness about them and she knew that no matter what happened on that boat, the man would take care of Susan.

"We'll leave you in his capable hands, then," said Rose with a tone that said anything less and he would have her to deal with.

"Nice to meet you, Mr. Legg," said Gia and held out her hand.

She tried not to breath in the strong smell of fish, but rather than shake her hand, he hugged her tightly until she was winded, then released her so quickly she nearly lost her balance.

"Let's be off then, love?" he said and peered down at Susan, then turned to her two friends. "We'll be back by six. God willing."

"Au revoir," Susan shouted, the wind whipping at her long skirt.

"We can wave from the shop," said Gia as Rose tugged at her arm. "Have fun, Susan."

"At least she'll be able to converse with the natives if they end up in France," said Rose with a hint of sarcasm.

Gia doubted they would end up in France, even if they got lost, as the land closest to them was Ireland.

Chapter 4

By five o'clock Gia was looking in her wardrobe and flinging coat hangers this way and that.

"I've nothing to wear," she said and saw David cringe.

"Just wear jeans," he said, hoping to be helpful.

"It's casual, then?"

David opened his mouth and closed it quickly, reminding Gia of a fish.

"Whatever you want," but he said it as a question as if stepping on to an old wooden bridge and wondering if it would hold.

But Gia hadn't noticed and her head was now in the depths of the built in wardrobe.

"What do you think?" she asked while holding up a black t-shirt with flowers embellished in rhinestones.

David didn't answer quickly enough and she threw it back, not bothering to return it to a hanger.

"A shirt. I'll wear a white shirt."

"Good idea," said David trying to sound cheery.

She turned to her husband, holding up a three quarter sleeved white shirt which she thought would look good with her dark blue jeans. She'd wear that necklace . . . but here her thoughts stopped as David finished buttoning up *his* white shirt.

"That won't do. We don't want to look like one of those unisex couples."

"I can change if you like," David offered, but Gia's white shirt had already landed on top of the black one.

"Pink. I've got one just like it in pink."

"I love you in pink," said David. Again, more of a question than a statement. "I'll just go and feed the dogs."

He backed out of the bedroom and the two dogs who had been sitting on their haunches watching the two of them as if at a tennis match, followed him.

Nothing was going right and Gia felt a lump in her throat, her eyes welled with unshed tears. The shirt was too tight across the bust so she opted for a cream colored, sleeveless top, beneath, leaving the shirt unbuttoned.

David stood in the doorway, looked at his watch, but didn't speak.

"What time is it?" asked Gia.

"Nearly six o'clock and our reservation —"

"Susan! I forgot Susan's boat was coming in at six. Will we have time to stop at the harbor?"

Rather than suggesting that they head straight to the restaurant, David pulled out his phone and with a sigh, requested that their reservation be changed to six thirty. He hoped they could get there and park the car in time.

David opened the car door for her, kissed her lightly on the cheek and was silent driving down to the harbor.

"Looks like they got in early," said Gia when she spotted the Mermaid tied up by the quay.

Her hand hovered on the door.

David looked at his watch and Gia leaned back.

"I'm sure she'll tell us all about it tomorrow," she said. "Let's go and eat."

They found a parking space and Gia was amazed at the way David maneuvered his burnt orange M.G. effortlessly into a small space. Parking, parallel or otherwise, had never been easy for Gia who had opted mostly for traveling by public transportation when she lived in London.

The sun was still shining and the evening warm. They walked toward the steps leading up to what had once been a small chapel. The stone and wrought iron fence flanked steps that led into the restaurant. On the ground floor was a bar, which stretched the length of the room, but they took the winding stone steps up to the mezzanine that had waist high glass and forded a view of the downstairs area.

"Everything okay?" David asked when Gia began studying the menu.

"Of course," she replied.

But everything wasn't okay. She didn't know how to navigate this new life she shared with David. She wasn't sure how she could be half of a couple. She'd been single for close to a third of a century.

"We haven't been here for ages," she said.

And they hadn't.

"Not since we got married," said David and he glanced at his wedding ring.

Was he having regrets?

She put down the menu and David slid his hand across the table and covered hers.

"Whatever it is," he raised his other hand palm out to silence the words that were forming in her mouth. "Whatever it is, Gia. We can work it out."

Gia bit the side of her mouth. David *would* say something like that. He thought everything was solvable.

"I love you," she whispered.

He simply smiled. The smile she loved. The lines by his eyes creased.

"Look!" he said when the moment had passed and he picked up the menu. "Chicken breast wrapped in ham and sautéed potatoes. Shall I order for us?"

She nodded, knowing that he would want seafood. The chicken was her favorite and he remembered.

But he hadn't said he loved her back. Her frown returned. Why hadn't he?

Then her thoughts turned to someone who kept popping into her mind at inopportune moments.

Meg.

Had Meg wondered the same thing? Perhaps she'd changed her mind about marriage. Perhaps she didn't think her fiancé loved her enough.

"Who was Meg engaged to?" she asked when their meals were served.

David held a king prawn on his fork. "Martyn Barker. Why?" He popped the prawn in his mouth and then twirled linguini on to his fork.

Below them a hen night had become rowdy. A chubby pink fairy hit a nurse with her wand.

"I've met him a few times," said David. "He seems like a nice enough bloke."

Gia didn't respond.

"He was on the opposing darts team. We won."

"You don't think he would kill her, then?"

"Gia."

"Okay. Sorry. I was just thinking."

She sliced the chicken breast.

"So, how's the training coming along?" she asked.

Gia barely listened as David told her about the minutes he'd shaved off his initial time, what his goals were, how much quicker he was getting at completing the course and how he'd made new friends.

It was a silly question. Anyone could kill. Anyone that is with enough anger or enough to lose. She had to widen her list of suspects.

"Swimming tomorrow?" she asked as David began to slow down his monolog.

"Only if . . ." he hesitated.

"It's fine with me. You're not going to be doing this forever, right. It's just another two weeks."

Once the two weeks were over, they could go back to their quiet evening walks with the dogs. The summer evenings drinking outside the King William and morning cuddles without David rushing off to run, bicycle or swim.

But as they returned to the car, Gia had more questions than answers. Was David still in love with her and who had hated Meg enough to kill her?

They drove home along country lanes, with hedges over spilling on to the roadway, like monsters with their arms outreached and lit only by the headlights of the car. David gripped her hand in his. He let it rest there in her lap.

"I love you, you know," he said without turning to her.

She watched his profile. His dark air, the shape of his ears, his mouth that kissed her so passionately. His hands, not calloused like those of a fisherman or farm worker, but of an accountant who used pens, and paper and a computer all day.

Her heart raced, her tummy gurgled and she thrust his hand aside.

"I think I'm going to be sick," she said unwinding the window and before he could stop the car, she retched out the window.

"I'm fine," she said when they pulled into the driveway. "I'll make some peppermint tea. That will help."

"Go and take a shower and I'll put the kettle on," David offered.

So much for a romantic evening. Romance, what does that even mean? Thought Gia. It happens before marriage, when couples are what Rose liked to call *courting*. But romance after marriage, you didn't witness it often.

She pulled back the soft sheets, the high thread count Egyptian cotton ones that Susan had splurged on for a wedding present, and glanced at the bedside table. Even her reading had changed. She used to wade through a stack of romance novels.

Novels with a hero. A tall, dark and handsome man who saved the lady in distress. Now all she read were mysteries. Mysteries about puzzles and murder.

"Drink this. It will make you feel better," said David handing her a familiar mug that Aunt Grace had once used.

She inhaled the smell of peppermint.

"When did I stop reading romance books?" she asked and drew her hand over the stack.

"I don't know. When we got married I guess. Better for me."

"Why?"

"Because no one could live up to the men in those books. Unless you want me to grow my hair?"

He shook his head as if dislodging hair from his shoulder.

She had to admit the covers were silly. Men with long hair and bare chests. Men she would never be attracted to in real life.

"Feeling better, love?" he asked and slipped off his shoes.

He sat next to her and wrapped his arm gently around her shoulders.

"What brought that on, Gia?"

"I don't know. Something in the chicken perhaps? Maybe not. There's something going around. Susan was sick all last week. Perhaps you should sleep in the other bedroom. You don't want to catch anything before your big race."

"Do you want me to?" he asked, his face had a puzzled expression.

"No. But I don't want to be selfish."

"Then, I'll stay right here. I'll just let the dogs out for a minute and I'll be right back."

But before David returned, Gia had sipped her tea and fallen asleep slumped on the pillows.

Chapter 5

"What do you mean, you've got an interview at a hotel in Truro?" asked Gia when Holly called her later that morning.

Already she was feeling tired. She'd woken up when David left, heading to the beach to swim and he promised to be back in time to help her prepare Sunday dinner. Both their parents would be arriving at noon and so far she hadn't got very far with the vegetables. David had put the beef in the oven, to roast, before he left.

"It's more money and they won't be a rowdy bunch like we get in the King William in the summer. It will be business men and people on holiday."

Gia felt her heart do a flip. Everything was changing and she didn't like it. She looked out the window at the fields behind her garden and the hotel in the distance which was busy in the summer with holidaymakers.

"Is there a man involved?" asked Gia.

Usually if Holly decided to make a change it concerned someone of the opposite sex.

There was no response and Gia feared the worst.

"Maximo,"

"And he is?" asked Gia knowing that someone of English descent wasn't likely to be on her friend's radar.

"French."

"I see," said Gia although she didn't see at all.

She glanced down at the potato she was peeling, as if it remained the only constant thing in her life with its bumps and uneven shape. She had been happy a year ago. Holly was as excited as she when Gia and David announced their engagement. Holly had been with her when she'd planned the wedding. Her friend had saved the day when disaster struck and here she was talking about moving to Truro.

Her best friend was moving.

"That's not all," said Holly.

"It isn't?"

Gia put down the potato peeler that she had never mastered and picked up a paring knife, slicing away at the potato and skin, which David said should be preserved because it contained all the goodness. Even her potato peeling skills were being questioned these days.

"I just want a change, Gia." said Holly.

"Oh."

A change from what? From her? From being her best friend?

"You can still come and have a drink when I'm at work."

"I'm not driving all the way to Truro every night. It's not like I can walk the dogs there is it?"

Gia regretted her outburst. The knife had slipped and nicked her finger and she let cold water from the tap run over it, watching blood mingle with the water and swirl down the drain.

"I'm sorry," she said and she was. Sorry for a lot of things. "I haven't spent much time with you, have I?"

"It's not that. Look, Maximo isn't even anyone important."

"Does he know that?"

Holly tended to flirt with everyone and made each man feel he was special, even when he wasn't.

"He's staying in Truro and called to let me know there was an opening for a bar maid at the hotel. That's all. I may not take it. I may not even be accepted," Holly gave a little laugh, but they both knew that Holly was a draw for any pub or bar.

Holly had a way with customers, made them feel at ease, poured drinks quickly and effortlessly and was always willing to listen. The chances of the manager not offering her a job was slim.

"You're right. We'll just wait and see what happens. Are you working today?" Gia asked.

"Nope. Barry's taking the lunch time shift and I'm off tonight too."

"I'm making a roast," said Gia and looked down at her finger now wrapped in a paper towel.

"You're cooking?"

"I'm trying to make an effort. David is swimming this morning as part of his training. I've invited mum and dad and Rose and Paul."

"A family affair, then," said Holly with a note of disappointment.

"You're as much part of the family as they are. You're my best friend. Come at twelve. We're having roast beef."

"And Yorkshire pudding?"

Darn she'd forgotten about that.

"Yes," she said and began flipping pages of Aunt Grace's cook book for the recipe.

Milk, eggs, flour. Yes, she had everything she needed for the batter which wasn't eaten as a pudding, but as part of a roast beef dinner, which was served at lunch time. Sometimes things that had been a tradition just didn't make sense when you stopped to look at the whole procedure.

"Okay," said Holly. "I'll be there. Mum and dad just got back from Tenerife this week. I've been eating frozen dinners."

This was something she had also eaten until David became part of her life. Then he had begun cooking for the two of them. Sometimes at his flat in Truro and sometimes at her house in Lowenna.

She'd better get a move on if she wanted to get the potatoes cooked in time.

Rose was the first to arrive and while David was in the shower and Paul had yet to walk across the driveway, she leaned close to Gia.

"No news, then?" she whispered.

"No, Rose. You'll be the first to know."

She wanted to ask Rose to stop asking. She wanted everyone to stop staring at her stomach and she wanted life to go back to normal.

"How's dinner coming along, then?" Rose asked. "I made a blackberry and apple pie for afters."

"Yum. You know it's my favorite," said Gia.

Gia draped her arm around Rose's shoulder and squeezed. She meant no harm, she wanted to be a grandmother. Her mother on the other hand wasn't the slightest bit interested. She didn't have a maternal bone in her body and probably hadn't had a second thought about David and Gia having a baby. At least she had no worries with her parents hounding her at the dinner table.

By the time everyone else had arrived, the whole house smelled of cabbage and Brussels sprouts.

Holly set the table, David poured drinks for everyone, and Rose hovered over the stove.

Gia's mum held out a box.

Felicity Matthews was glamorous with bleach blond hair, perfectly applied makeup so thick that it sometimes looked like a mask. She wore jeans with a perfect crease and a tailored lavender colored shirt.

"Just a little present," she said. "Something I found that I think you'll love."

The kitchen, which usually only had two occupants was becoming increasingly crowded. Rose and David stood by the stove. Paul was trying to squash himself by the pantry door and her dad stood in the hall doorway. Her mum stood in the center of the kitchen still holding the box.

"Yoo hoo," shouted Holly.

She had stuck her head through the serving hatch, which was the size of a television, between the living room and the kitchen. "Why don't you come in here?"

43

Holly looked at Gia's mum who nodded and thrust the box into Gia's hand.

"I'll cut the meat while you're serving the vegetables," said David to Gia when her mum and dad had vacated the kitchen.

"I hope the Yorkshire pudding has risen. Sometimes it gets a bit deflated," said Gia, shaking the white box and wondering if her mother had bought her a shirt.

"It's when your oven isn't hot enough," said Rose.

David opened the oven door and Gia peered over his shoulder. The Yorkshire pudding had risen so much it was stuck to the top of the oven. David took out the potatoes while he scraped the pudding from the oven ceiling and then took out the roast beef surrounded by carrots, parsnips and onions all cooked in the drippings from the meat.

"The potatoes aren't done," said Rose plunging a fork into them. "Leave them in a bit longer and you can have them tomorrow," she said. "Where's the gravy?"

Gia had forgotten the gravy. The Yorkshire pudding was ruined and the potatoes weren't done.

"It's all right, love," said Rose. "Paul, she shouted. "Pop back home and get a box of potato flakes and the Bisto. Gia, put the kettle on, we'll get this done in no time."

"Why don't you leave them to it," said Holly still peering through the serving hatch. "Come and have a glass of wine."

"I don't think I'm cut out to be married," said Gia when she walked into the living room and slumped into a chair.

"Of course you are. That's the silliest thing I've ever heard. I bet if you ask Rose, she'll tell you some stories of things that happened when she was first married to David's dad."

Gia blinked back tears. She was hating this roller coaster of emotions and wondered if it was too early for the change. Did anyone experience menopause in their early thirties?

"Aren't you going to open the present your mum bought you?" asked Holly.

Gia touched the blue and pink ribbon, and ran her hand over the shirt size box. Her mum rarely thought of her, let alone bought her presents.

"I can't wait," said her mum from the doorway.

"Wait for what?" asked Gia unwrapping the tissue.

"You can take back whichever one you don't want. I left the receipt in there," said Felicity Matthews and gripped her husband's hand, then released it just as quickly.

As Gia opened the box both she and Holly gasped. For once, Gia was speechless and on the floor, where the open box had spilled, was a pink baby outfit and also one in blue.

"I found it in a little shop in Polperro," said her mum, but Gia wasn't listening and she doubted her mum had noticed that she had stood, leaving the baby clothes on the floor.

"I'll go and help in the kitchen," she said when she got to the door.

But she headed straight for her bedroom and David found her sitting on the bed staring at the blue and yellow wallpaper.

"What's the matter?" he asked. "Dinner is fine. You did a great job."

"Mum," Gia sighed from deep within.

"What did she do now?" David draped his arm around her shoulders and gave her a hug.

"She bought baby clothes."

"Well, aren't we going to have a baby someday?"

"But I'm not pregnant now."

David obviously didn't get it. He didn't understand the pressure, didn't feel the need to please everyone and it wasn't his body that was in question.

"I'll be out in a minute, you go and help Rose," said Gia, feeling that she was not needed in the kitchen or apparently anywhere else at the moment.

"This is delicious," said her dad as he cut into a soggy piece of Yorkshire pudding. "And the meat's very tender."

Gia's dad was very like David in temperament. He was buffer between Felicity and her daughter.

He was a slender man, the same height as her mother, both being five feet, ten. He had bushy eyebrows, thin lips and deep brown eyes. Gia and her dad shared the same nose genes.

"Have you talked to Susan, Rose," Gia asked. "The Mermaid had already docked when we got there Saturday night."

"No. I doubt she caught anything. She was popping those sea sickness pills like crazy all afternoon."

"Kwells?" asked Holly. "I think you're only supposed to take one every six hours and not more than three in a day."

"What she wants with a fisherman, I'll never know."

"Won't catch me in a boat," said Gia's dad. "Not after last year."

Both John Trewellyn and her dad had been collecting cockles last year and went in the water to retrieve John's boat that had drifted away. He'd ended up in bed for days.

"Staying firmly on dry land," added her dad. "Looks like you've been keeping busy, Paul. That shed of yours won't hold much more."

Gia dropped her fork and when she leaned down to retrieve it, she noticed Paul was holding Rose's hand underneath the table. They'd only been married two years, how did they keep the spark alive?

"Did you hear what's happening up at the manor?" asked Paul.

"Meg's death, you mean?" asked Holly.

"I'd forgotten that Meg and Collin lived on a tenant farm on the Glasten estate," said Rose.

"No, not that," said Paul.

"Then what?" his wife asked.

"The estate is being sold," said Paul.

"But those families have lived there for generations. Some for over a hundred years," said Rose.

46

Gia's mum lowered her fork. "Why wouldn't they buy the farm? Doesn't make sense to rent somewhere for that long."

"It was different years ago. The manor took care of their tenants. But it's not that way any longer. Mr. Gillard provided for the tenants in his will. No one thought there was a danger of it being sold. But now he's gone who knows what will happen."

"Where would they go?" Gia's dad asked Rose.

"There aren't many places to rent any more. Houses around here have been sold up for second homes or rented out to people on holiday. Locals have difficulty renting somewhere."

"Ten million," said Paul. "That's what the college is expecting to get."

"I always thought Mrs. Gillard was the lady of the manor," said Holly.

"No," said David. "It was left to a charitable trust, a college in Hampshire. And the will, Mr. Gillard's will, was supposed to insure that the rent collected was added to the trust and used to maintain the village. It was in the paper a few years ago. Mr. Gillard paid fifteen thousand pounds for the estate in the 1930s."

It always amazed Gia just how much David knew about the goings on in the village and surrounding countryside. She supposed that being an accountant he found out all kinds of interesting tidbits.

"So," said Holly. "Collin lost his sister and home all in one fell swoop."

"I wonder if there's a connection?" asked Gia and they all turned to her.

"Don't get involved, love," said Paul.

Gia thought about Meg. She would have fought for their family farm. Her parents and their parents before them had been brought up there. Had she perhaps found a loophole that would prevent the sale? She wondered if she could find a copy of the will and take it to Mr. Alderton, the solicitor who had helped her with her aunt's will. Perhaps she could help Collin.

"And Collin is a suspect in his sister's murder?" asked Rose.

"I can't see Collin hurting his sister," said Holly. "But he wasn't the only one who didn't want Meg to marry."

"Oh?"

"Her fiancé's family is pretty well to do. They wanted him to insist on a pre-nuptial agreement and Meg wasn't having any of that."

"I don't blame her," said Gia. "It's like drawing up divorce papers before you're even married. Not a good way to show you're committed."

"Gia wouldn't sign one either," said David and everyone laughed.

It wasn't like either of them had great wealth. Gia did have her inheritance that Aunt Grace had left and David had the money he'd saved hoping to buy a house of his own someday, but they'd pooled all their money and put it in an account in both their names. She trusted David.

"Can you give me a lift to the knitting circle tomorrow?" Rose asked Gia while the men discussed money matters.

"I have all my squares ready," said Gia.

The ladies of the knitting circle made squares that Rose put together and they gave the blankets to the residents at a local nursing home.

"Why don't you come with us, Felicity?" asked Rose.

Gia cringed.

Her mum slowly shook her head. "I'm all fingers and thumbs."

Felicity had been invited to the knitting circle on more than one occasion and Gia guessed it wasn't lack of creativity that prevented her mother from joining the ladies, but more of a feeling that she was too good for the likes of the local women.

"I'm not good at making things," she continued. "I'm good at shopping though." She glanced over at the baby outfits that had been stuffed into the box and were on a chair by the fireplace.

"Everyone ready for apple and blackberry pie?" asked Rose when Holly and Gia began clearing plates.

Rose's pie was sure to be perfect. She was an excellent cook and perhaps Gia should ask her to teach her a few things rather than feeling threatened by Rose's cooking skills that David had grown up with.

But when the pie was served, Gia found that the apples were not soft and luscious as they usually were. Perhaps she had only been focusing on accomplishments and not failures of her friends. She didn't think it was a big deal, just like they probably didn't when her potatoes weren't cooked and the Yorkshire pudding was stuck to the top of the oven.

"No problem," said Rose, scooping the plate away from Gia. "We'll just pop it in the microwave."

There was always a solution to a problem. You just had to search for what it was. Surrounded by friends and family, even her mother, was a good place to be. She looked out the window at the beach and the tide rolling along the sand. Seagulls whooped and whooshed in the sky, and she heard them screech occasionally as they passed overhead. Life was good. She reached over and squeezed David's hand. She wanted to stay in this cocoon forever with those dearest to her.

Then Holly spoke. "Did Gia tell you I've applied for a job in Truro?"

Chapter 6

"All clear," said Rose when she climbed into Gia's green Volkswagen Golf.

They both looked toward the car park. Did Rose expect for another body to appear? But Rose was looking in the other direction.

"You can pull out. It's all clear," she repeated.

Rose wasn't the best passenger. She'd failed miserably at learning to drive, but liked to offer help to anyone else who was behind the steering wheel. Despite their relatively slow and short trip to the village hall, Rose was gripping the handle so tight her knuckles whitened.

They parked by the pavement leading to the church and walked behind to the village hall. St. Bartholomew's was a Norman style building. Large blocks of stone supported stained glass windows of the gothic structure. They sparkled in the sunlight, lights dancing through the biblical scenes. Giovanna gazed beyond the church to the village hall nestled among trees. She had been there many times for weddings, dances and jumble sales.

"Lovely bell," said Rose which she felt she had to comment on each time they passed the church.

Due to the contents of an old deed, Gia had found herself responsible for the purchase of a new church bell. There was something to be said for a new country that didn't have deeds and records going back hundreds of years. You never knew what you were buying when you bought a house in England and it often included more than the plot of land you could see.

Mrs. Jones, the policeman's wife, was the first person they spotted. But before she could engage them in negative conversation, Rose and Gia headed to the kitchen where Rose left a Victoria sponge cake with raspberry jam oozing from the center and powdered sugar on the top in a lace design.

"Looks delicious," said Gia.

"See what I did on the top?" asked Rose. "I saw it in Ladies Weekly. You put a doily on the cake, then put powdered sugar in a sieve and sprinkle it on top. Makes a lovely design. I got a new chicken recipe too. I'll make it this week and let you and David have some."

Maybe that's what she needed to do. Look at women's magazines. She'd stop at Trewellyn's later today.

Iris Trewellyn was the next person they saw.

"Have you talked to Susan?" she asked.

"We haven't seen her since Saturday afternoon. Did something happen on the boat?" asked Gia.

"She caught a tuna," said Iris.

"But there aren't any tuna around here," observed Rose.

"Well, she caught one. John and Mr. Legg are going to see if they can get a commercial fishing license to fish for tuna."

"And Susan caught it?" asked Rose.

"Not exactly," said Iris. "I'll let her tell you the story."

Of course, with Susan there was always a story. She was sure to have a tale to tell, thought Gia.

"I'll go and set up the chairs," said Gia and walked into the hall where ladies had already begun to pull out chairs and place them in a circle. A table had an assortment of squares which Rose would take home and put together to make a blanket.

The old village hall that abutted the church had wooden floors the color of toffee. It smelled musty with a hint of lemon oil. At the end was a stage with red curtains that had once been plush velvet, but now had very little sheen to them.

"Still no sign of Susan," said Rose. "I wonder if we should call her."

But Susan walked in before Rose could pull her phone from her pocket.

She walked slowly and her face had an ashen look.

"Are you all right?" asked Gia. She pulled out a chair for Susan.

"You look awful," said Rose.

"We heard you caught a tuna," said Gia.

Susan slumped into a chair. "My rod did. I left it hanging there and when I woke up, there was this big fish in the boat."

"You were asleep?" asked Rose. "You didn't notice them hauling that thing in?"

"I didn't know you were only supposed to take one of those tablets. I've been sleeping on and off since Saturday. That is except when I got sick." she turned to Gia. "I think I had a tummy bug again."

This was good news to Gia. Perhaps it was just a bug that she had too and all her symptoms weren't early menopause. But then sickness wasn't part of it anyway, was it?

"Are you feeling better?" Susan asked Gia.

"Yes."

And she was. She had felt fine yesterday, even after the dinner of roast beef and the delicious apple and blackberry pie. Perhaps it had been something that had now flushed through her system.

"Percy said he'd take me out again, but I mustn't take those pills."

"Sometimes your body changes. You might not need to take any sea sickness tablets," offered Gia.

"Craziness, that's what I call it," said Rose. "Why would you want to go out on one of those little boats."

The three of them turned to Iris whose husband went out on a little boat most days.

"Percy Legg is a good fisherman," said Iris. "Susan will be safe with him."

But Rose wasn't so sure any more. Like Gia's dad she preferred to have her feet firmly on the ground.

The hall buzzed with conversation. Talk was mostly about the weather and the mess caused by the foam on the beach. Some ladies provided bed and breakfast in their homes in the summer and they complained that there had been cancelled bookings after the frothy beach was televised on the news. Tourism was a big industry along the Cornish coast in the summer.

"Better if they stayed away," said Mrs. Jones. "I bet that mess was caused by them holidaymakers."

Susan opened her mouth to give them information she'd learned from the internet, but Rose nudged her and she quickly closed it.

"No point saying anything," whispered Rose. "She's going to complain about something. Best let her go on about that for a few days."

What Mrs. Jones didn't remember is that before hotels and tourism had come to the area, their roads were in bad repair, there was nowhere to park, no public toilets and few restaurants. Despite the crowds for a few months in the summer, the locals were able to take advantage of the improvements for most of the year.

"And those dogs," said Mrs. Jones and glared at Gia. "Always running on the beach and leaving their doo-doos behind."

"Not in the summer," Gia felt she should stick up for her four legged friends. "The dogs aren't allowed on the beach in the summer."

"There was one on Friday morning, just running around free as you please," said Mrs. Jones. "I called my husband." She said this as if it was the worst threat that she could offer for a misdemeanor, but most of the group felt little respect for P.C. Jones who had the same sour attitude his wife had.

"What color was it?" asked Gia.

"Black and white," Mrs. Jones said.

Gia guessed it was Bailey that Mrs. Jones had seen. Did Mrs. Jones discover Meg too? The disgruntled woman soon clarified who had found Collin's sister.

"My husband was first on the scene," she added. "He chased the dog and found that woman."

"You mean Meg Penhallow," said Gia who hated that Collin's sister was now only referred to as the body, the victim or that woman.

"That bunch up at the manor won't be there for much longer anyway," said Mrs. Jones "And then where will we be?"

"Be?" asked Susan lowering her knitting needles.

"That woman and her brother had lived there all their lives. Their father and his father before him too. All those tenants were part of the village and they're being turfed out for what? So some rich people can come down from up north and have a nice little holiday in the countryside. Who's going to take care of the village when people are coming and going every Sunday, I ask you?" She didn't wait for a response. "The villagers. All those tenant farmers. They were the ones who repaired fences, trimmed hedges, took care of the village green. Their families were born here." She turned and cast her eye on anyone who she suspected might have been born somewhere other than Cornwall. "And dead and buried in the chapel graveyard." She took a sharp intake of breath. "But it makes you wonder what that woman was up to."

"Up to?" asked Susan and wound the pink wool around her needle.

"Well, you don't get knocked on the head for no reason."

Mrs. Jones having finished her tirade, leaned back in her chair, and adjusted the knitting in her lap.

She had a point. Was Meg up to something she shouldn't have been?

But Mrs. Jones wasn't finished.

"If she was getting the folks all riled up, then whoever is buying the estate wouldn't want any bad news getting out. That wouldn't look good for when they started renting cottages out to holidaymakers now would it?"

"It would come up on Boogle," said Susan.

"Exactly," said Mrs. Jones, but her face was puzzled.

"She means Google," offered Rose who probably had no idea what it meant.

She had a point. If someone did a search on the property they would see that there had been problems among the locals. But would the buyers be angry enough to kill her? And why leave her in a car park? Surely there was enough land to bury someone on if you wanted to commit murder.

"Handing out flyers she was," said Mrs. Jones.

Iris who was the diplomatic one of the group jumped in. "Rose made a Victoria sponge," she said. "Very pretty pattern on the top with the sugar," she nodded toward Rose and smiled. "Shall we take a break, ladies and have a cup of tea?"

"If you have any finished squares, leave them on the table," said Rose. We'll have quite a few blankets by Christmas to take up to the Honeysuckle Rest Home.

The tone lightened with talk of Christmas which was five months away, and more news batted about than the local paper, The Westerner, had room for.

"Did you hear about that woman over in St. Agnes?" asked a blond woman wearing a low cut sun dress with her bosom barely contained. "She lost her house."

"Lost as in mislaid it?" asked Rose sarcastically.

"No, silly," said the woman and wound lime green chunky yarn around an equally thick wooden needle.

Gia watched Rose lower her head and glare at the voluptuous woman who was oblivious to the stare.

Rose wouldn't be too happy at trying to incorporate such a bright color in her traditional colored blanket, and the woman was using needles that were somewhat larger than the size eight that Rose insisted on. Rose had consented, reluctantly, to the circle referring to the metric size of four millimeters, but the size the woman was using were not correct by any stretch of the imagination and to be called silly was going to get a response.

She watched Rose's chest puff up and Gia jumped in to avoid her friend voicing her thoughts.

"Where was this?" Gia asked.

"Up behind the car park. Where the library is," said the woman. "I was up there yesterday and the policeman told me the woman that lived there came home and her living room was gone."

Susan, who was looking much better after a cup of tea, chose to clarify. "It's the sink holes. There's a chimney for the mine shaft up there so you know there are tunnels all beneath that area. There was a garden up there last year that had a forty foot tree in the front. When the family got up one morning all they could see was branches."

One more thing to give her nightmares, thought Gia. When she was young she often dreamed that the cliffs would crumble away and she'd wake up to a sea view closer than she wanted. But she hadn't had nightmares for a long time. Although she had experienced restless nights lately. She vowed to take the dogs for longer walks. Breathing in the sea air seemed to do wonders for a good night's sleep.

"You daydreaming again?" asked Rose looking down at the strand of wool in Gia's hand. "If you don't get moving, you won't have anything to show for this morning."

Rose was casting off her second square.

"What is wrong with you?" asked Rose when she left the knitting circle with Susan and Gia.

"Me?" asked Susan.

"No. I'll never figure out what's wrong with you," said Rose, but she didn't sound unkind. "You're away with the fairies most of the time."

"I don't know," said Gia honestly. "Perhaps it's this whole business with Meg."

"But you hardly knew her," said Rose.

Rose was right. She hadn't known Meg very well. Their paths hadn't crossed often, but they were close in age and somehow it made life seem more delicate, more uncertain.

"Your dad looks good," said Rose changing the subject.

After his illness in December, they had all worried that her dad would be in a weakened state, but he seemed to have bounced back.

"He won't be going out looking for cockles again, though," said Gia.

"And your mum . . . ?" Rose left the question hanging.

Surprisingly, her mum had settled into life in Lowenna. Gia had thought after a few months she would be off somewhere else. Before Aunt Grace had died, her mum announced that it would be better for her dad's health if they moved to the Sunshine State and they sold their London antique shop and moved across the Atlantic, ending up on the Florida peninsular. They seemed relatively happy there until an alligator decided to share their garden and that was the end of that adventure.

"She's taken up golf," said Gia.

"With your dad?" asked Susan.

"No. She's joined some women's club. She likes it because she can wear little golf outfits with pastel colored caps, and sip cocktails in the club bar afterwards."

"Well as long as she's found somewhere to fit in," said Rose sounding grateful that it wasn't their knitting circle that she'd set her sights on. Felicity Matthews had made it perfectly clear that sitting with people and knitting for a morning was not to her liking.

Golf seemed the ideal choice. As long as it was a sport where she didn't have to sweat, her makeup and hair stayed in place and she could parade around in a new outfit, her mum was happy.

Gia thought again about the gift her mum had left. It was odd. She had never shown any interest when Gia's friends had married and visited with their new babies, never been interested in anything maternal for that matter. As a child it was either her dad or Aunt Grace she went to with a scraped knee or the problems of a teenager, but never her mother who was the sun in the family and her family the stars that revolved around her, but never touching.

"I'll pop in and see them later, I think David said he's training tonight," said Gia.

"He seems to be taking this race seriously," said Rose. "Another two weeks and it will be over," she added.

What she was expecting to happen then Gia wasn't sure. But she did wonder if David would continue running and joining his friends training for another competition.

The afternoon was slow. Very few customers came into the shop on Mondays. Saturday was changeover day and tourists either went home or arrived, taking a day or two to settle in before wandering around the shops and visiting local tourist haunts.

Gia called Mrs. Rundle to tell her she'd found the Woodland Hunting Dogs plate and saucer she was looking for. Mrs. Rundle wasn't too pleased about the price, but Gia didn't think any amount would have been suitable for the ex-mayor. Gia placed the order and agreed to call when it came in.

She phoned her mum and offered to pick up fish and chips on her way to her mum and dad's house. Felicity wasn't very keen on fish and chips but her dad loved them. Her mum consented only because it meant she wouldn't have to concern herself with cooking dinner.

After dropping Rose at home and feeding Canute and Daisy, Gia drove up the hill. Around the bend with views of rolling hills and a neat back garden, was a small house that her parents' had bought when they returned to England from Florida. For a variety of reasons, none of which made sense to Gia, her parents had chosen to move to Cornwall rather than returning to London. She doubted that her mum's choice of location had anything to do with being near her only daughter.

She noticed the paving stones shaped like an alligator that Holly had given them had been disposed of. Her mother didn't think it was as funny as Holly did. An alligator in the swimming pool was one of the reasons her mother had given for leaving Florida.

Her dad hugged her a little longer than usual and she wondered if her mum had been finding fault with Gia before she arrived. He always seemed to know when she needed that extra bit of sympathy even if it was something she had neither heard nor witnessed.

She followed him into the house. The stairs and hallway had a plush pale gray carpet with walls of white that showed a tint of blue during the daylight hours. There weren't many family photographs or anything to denote the house was anything, but for show.

While they sat at the table in the kitchen, Gia looked through the patio doors toward the garden. She had liked the way it was a jumble of flowers with haphazard lawn edges and a rustic fence, but now it was linear with nothing left to nature. Each plant or bush was placed in a design.

Her dad was liberally shaking the malt vinegar on both his fish and chips and her mother cringed as if she'd unexpectedly taken a bite of a sour lemon.

Gia noticed brochures for a retirement community on the table.

"What's this," she asked.

"Nothing," said her mum.

But her dad pushed them toward her and raised his bushy eyebrows.

"Your mum thinks we might do better in a retirement community," he said with little enthusiasm.

"They're building one up behind the sand dunes," said her mum. "They'll have their own private golf course, community center, swimming pool and we'll be able to mix with people like us. Sandy Dunes Retirement Community."

Gia doubted there was anyone who could be like her mother.

"You don't like living here?" Gia asked.

"Your mother . . ." her dad began, but simply shook his head and took his time slicing his fish as if he were a heart surgeon.

"We get fumes here," said her mother. "From the traffic." She nodded toward the road which was busy in the summer months.

Having lived in London, Gia didn't think any roads here could compare to the exhaust fumes and industrial smoke that they had breathed in for years. Of course, her mother would find an excuse like she was a martyr and not doing something selfishly.

And then it came. "Your father's health," she said.

Her father simply slumped his shoulders. He wasn't one to disagree with her mother, wasn't one to make waves and wasn't one to voice his wants or concerns.

They made eye contact. Both father and daughter knew who wanted to make a change.

"We need to mix with the right people," said Felicity and made a grimace with each bite of fish.

Obviously the right people wouldn't be eating meals from the fish and chip shop. And definitely wouldn't be like her husband's family or friends.

When Gia had told her mother that David had asked her to marry him, Felicity had asked why she wasn't marrying that nice solicitor. But Alan hadn't been nice, had cheated on her and had only wanted to marry because it was a stipulation for receiving his inheritance. Her mother hadn't looked at any of those things. All she heard was an estate in Scotland, wealthy parents, a standing in the community. David was a wonderful husband, Rose a great mother-in-law and she wouldn't want to change that for all the tea in China.

"Why? Why aren't you ever happy, mother," said Gia and then regretted voicing her concerns out loud.

"Now, love," said her dad.

Her mother simply stared at her and didn't immediately respond.

Through the silence Gia heard the tic-toc of a cuckoo clock on the wall. After a few beats, her mother spoke.

"I could ask you the same thing."

Of course she would turn it around into something her daughter had done.

"Moping around because you're not pregnant. Go to the doctors and get whatever the problem is sorted out."

"I'm not moping." Gia's voice had risen and her dad rested his hand on her arm. "Look at this lovely park," he said, pointing to the brochure where children played on swings and slides.

"You won't be able to walk to the shops," said Gia which she knew her dad liked to do.

"It will be fine, love. Really."

Her dad was once again resigned to be uprooted. At least his wife wasn't moving him to another country, moving him away from his friends and their only daughter. He often got together with Paul Lanner, and John Trewellyn to play poker or popped into Lowenna Antiques for a cup of tea.

She looked again at the brochure, at the cover, at the map inside.

"It's the manor!" she said. "This is what they're going to do to the manor? You didn't say anything yesterday when we were talking about it."

"We didn't realize it was the same place," said her dad.

So, they would be removing families from the tenant farms to put in a golf course and rows of houses that all looked the same.

"We won't even have to mow the grass," said her dad. "They have someone taking care of the gardens."

"You'll have to pay for that," snapped Gia.

"We know," fired back her mother. "This is exactly why I didn't want to say anything. I told you, George."

"Look, love," said her dad, his voice barely a whisper. "We're not . . ." he looked at his wife who raised her eyebrow. "I'm not getting any younger. It would be nice for someone else to take care of everything."

"So, they'll pull all those old farms down?" asked Gia.

"No. I think the plan is to rent them out in the summer. This development is going to be on the agricultural land."

"It will cost millions," said Gia.

"It's a French company," said her mother as if this explained all the cost.

"It's not definite," said her dad.

He opened a can of beer and carefully poured it into a glass, then returned to eating his fish and chips.

"I'm not hungry anymore," said her mother and pushed her plate away from her.

Had everyone gone crazy? At least Rose and Paul were settled. She didn't expect them to pick up and move any time soon. She would have to be more patient with her mother. Let's face it she wouldn't be able to change her and for her father's sake, she needed to try and make amends.

"So, you've joined the golf club?" she asked more enthusiastically than she felt.

Her mother looked at her, staring into her eyes as if deciding if this was another criticism or if her daughter was interested in her latest hobby. She obviously decided it was the latter. She smiled, but her face barely moved and Gia wondered if it was more than the makeup that caused the effect. Perhaps the result of Botox or even plastic surgery.

"Persephone Benton-Smythe has been introducing me to the members. We had cocktails together on Friday."

Gia had long known that anything ending with Smythe was a rich person's way of disguising the common name of Smith. Where the hyphenated names came from she never knew.

"I haven't heard of her," said Gia.

"Oh, she's on a member of the Fox and Hounds," said her mother.

"Sounds like a pub," mumbled George with a mouth full of fish.

Felicity ignored him and turned to Gia. "You probably don't run in those circles."

"You do know that fox hunting has been banned?" said Gia.

"They do drag hunting. The dogs follow a scent, not the actual fox. I'm sure it's a lot of fun."

"Tally ho and all that," said Gia.

Again, Felicity ignored the sarcasm. "Persephone Benton-Smythe lives with her husband in those big houses, just outside Lowenna. The ones that look like French chateaux. He's in finance you know."

Both Gia and her dad shrugged. Apparently neither of them knew that Mrs. Persephone Benton-Smythe's husband was *in finance*.

They had got on a better footing and Gia decided to finish up her fish and chips and leave while the going was good. She glanced back at the brochure.

"If it's only for retirement homes, then why would they have a playground?" she asked.

Her mother smiled. "For the grandchildren of course."

Chapter 7

Holly had persuaded Gia to join her while she visited the hotel for her interview with the manager. While she waited, sipping club soda and orange juice, Gia made notes on changes needed for the shop. It was getting crowded and she planned to ask Paul if he would put in some more shelves in the storage area behind a curtain at the back of the shop.

She looked up to see a man not much taller than she and judged him to be about the same age. He showed a look of recognition when he spotted her.

What was it her mum had always told her? Keep talking until you found out where you knew them from. She was sure she hadn't met him before though.

But he put her mind to rest immediately.

"You must be Gia," he said with an accent that was distinctly French.

"Maximo?" she asked deciding that it must be Holly's boyfriend.

"I prefer Max," he said and pulled out a scarlet leather tub chair with a curved back blending into the armrests. "May I?"

Gia could see why Holly was attracted to him. He had almost black hair and dark eyebrows, and his eyes were a deep blue. He had a self assured way about him without being arrogant.

"You're the friend of the lovely Holly," he said as if she were equally lovely.

It had been a long time since anyone had flirted with her and she liked the way he made eye contact and held her gaze while he was talking to her. Did David ever do that? She couldn't remember. They were barely even in the same room together these days except to sleep.

"Holly is meeting with the manager," said Gia.

"Can I get you another while we're waiting," he asked nodding toward her half empty glass.

Before she could respond he had risen and ordered drinks for both of them at the bar.

"So, you're stealing my friend away from Lowenna," said Gia.

"Hardly stealing. Don't you think this would be nice for her? I've put in a good word that's all."

And it was nice. No stale beer smell hit you when walking in the door. There were no stains on the floor and even the glass topped tables had no rings on them from overflowing drinks. They sparkled. The room smelled new, chemical smells of new paint and new wooden flooring. Behind the contemporary bar of black wood there were no hooks for the pewter tankards that the locals preferred. Instead there were built-in shelves displaying expensive liquors reflected in a mirror reaching the ceiling. Bar stools had backs and on the edge of the bar was a bouquet of red flowers in a tall vase. Above the bar hung five cylindrical lights from silver rods.

She could imagine Holly here, but would she be happy?

Happy wasn't a word she would use. It was cold and uninviting. Business men and women would come and go and there would be no chance for Holly to get to know them. Holly thrived on helping people and becoming part of the group. But Gia said none of this.

"There isn't a dart board," she blurted.

Maximo leaned back and laughed. Even his laugh seemed to have an accent.

"You English and your darts," he said.

And right there, she knew that if Holly did take the job, did continue seeing Maximo, it wouldn't be for long. This wasn't what Holly would feel comfortable with after a while.

Maximo stood when Holly entered the room and raised his eyebrow in question.

"The manager said he wanted me to do a trial run on Saturday afternoon, but it looks good. I think he liked me."

"And who wouldn't," said Max, kissing not her cheek, nor her lips, but her hand.

Holly grinned.

He moved toward the bar, but Holly put her arm out. "Don't get me a drink. We need to be getting back," she said.

His smiled faded, disappointment evident.

"Until this evening, then?" he asked.

Gia stood too and wondered if she should leave and give them time alone, but Holly was already walking toward the door.

"So, what do you think?" she asked when they were both in her forest green Jeep.

"It's very clean," said Gia.

"No. Not the hotel. Maximo?"

Holly wound her way around the double roundabout and headed out of town.

"He's very nice," was all Gia could think to say. "Good looking," she added absently and watched the river disappear behind a supermarket.

"And that accent," said Holly waving her hand in front of her face as if she were about to swoon.

"Yes, the accent is a big plus."

David would say he sounded effeminate and not very manly, but Gia could see how attractive Maximo was. Not unlike the men on the cover of her romance books whom she would never dream of going out with, but were nice to look at nevertheless.

"What's wrong?" asked Holly taking her eyes off the road briefly and turning to Gia.

If Holly wanted to work at a hotel in Truro, then she needed to be more enthusiastic, more encouraging.

"Nothing," Gia said. "Nothing's wrong."

Before they could talk further, Holly spotted a motor cycle in her rear view mirror and hugged the road to let him pass.

"That's Collin Penhallow," Holly said.

"Does he ride that all the time?"

"Yes. They didn't have a car."

"How can you run a farm without a car?" asked Gia.

"They had workers helping them."

"I guess that takes him off the suspect list, then," said Gia.

"Why?"

"You couldn't move a dead body on a motor bike and I don't think Meg was killed in the car park."

"How do you figure these things out?" asked Holly.

Gia shrugged. She didn't know, but she had a feeling that Meg had been dumped there. But what about the dog? How had Bailey got to the beach? And Collin could have had an accomplice.

"By the way, I met Mrs. Gillard from the manor while I was waiting for the manager," said Holly.

Of course Mrs. Gillard would be a patron of an upscale hotel bar and not one of the local pubs. Holly was moving in different circles these days.

"Is it Lady Gillard?" asked Gia.

"No," Holly let out a little laugh. "Her husband was a school teacher. He worked at the college in Hampshire that's the trustee for the estate. She's as down to earth as they come."

"He didn't leave the estate to his wife?"

"The trust is supposed to make sure everyone can stay there, including his wife. They both loved that little hamlet. He bought it for fifteen thousand pounds eons ago. Anyway," Holly continued before Gia could respond. "They have cooking classes up at the manor. There's a big kitchen and she's allowed her cook to do classes there."

"Nice," said Gia without much enthusiasm.

"I thought we could go," said Holly. She slowed down when a tractor pulled out and they waited until he crossed the road and drove into a field.

"We?"

"Well, you said you wanted to learn some new things and I'd like to see around the manor so what about it?"

Gia looked out the window, at the fields behind the Cornish walls with haphazard stone and slate shaped in a chevron pattern. She watched the sheep lazily grazing in the field and spotted birds soar with the thermal winds.

"I'll go with you," Gia said, but didn't turn from the window.

"Great. I'll let you know when."

While she sat in Rose and Paul Lanner's living room drinking tea and eating another slice of bakewell tart, savoring the almond flavor mingled with raspberry jam, she watched a family with two small children carrying bundled towels and a picnic basket, pass the house on the way to the beach. The wind whipped away the hat of one of the girls and the man chased after it, followed by his daughter. Would David be a good father, would they have family outings or would David work later hours like many new fathers tended to do? Whether this was a drive for men to take care of their families financially or to avoid going home to noise and chaos, she wasn't sure, but it seemed to happen to a lot of her friends.

Rose's living room was the same size as the one across the driveway, but with wallpaper of large print scarlet and orange flowers it seemed smaller. The room hadn't changed for as long as Gia could remember. It was a cozy room with oversized comfortable furniture facing a fireplace. A small table of pine wood and two Windsor chairs sat by the window and she could imagine Rose and Paul eating breakfast while looking at the sea view.

"What wrong, love?" asked Paul when he came back with a fresh pot of tea. "You look so in the doldrums lately."

Gia watched Paul as he sat. His bald head shined as if he'd just polished it that morning. His faded jeans hugged his portly waist but hung loosely around thin legs. On his feet were moccasin leather slippers.

"I'm okay," said Gia.

"No. You're not."

Paul put down the pot and hovered his hand over Gia's.

"I know everyone is expecting me to get pregnant, but what if it never happens?"

Gia thought it strange that she could always confide in Paul and could tell him things that she didn't share with Rose, especially as he had been a confirmed bachelor until his sixties and never experienced the family or dating problems she had dealt with the past few years. Paul never looked at her as if he were judging her, but offered kindly advice and encouragement and he listened. That's what she loved about him – he listened.

"Oh, love. It will," said Paul, but didn't grip her hand.

"But you don't know. No one knows," said Gia. "And everyone —"

"They just want to let you know that they're excited for you. They want to share it with you."

"But, Rose –"

"You know Rose wants grandchildren?"

Gia did.

"Do you want me to talk to her?" asked Paul.

Did she? She doubted it would help. Rose didn't understand.

"She probably didn't know it was bothering you," said Paul. "You know she can be a bit insensitive, but she doesn't mean any harm. I'll ask her not to talk about it."

They made eye contact and both laughed. Asking Rose not to talk about something was like trying to repair a hole in the harbor wall with chewing gum.

It didn't matter what Rose or anyone else said, it was what they were thinking and she would always know it.

"Perhaps you and David need a few days on your own. Why don't you go and book yourselves into a nice hotel or something?"

"David's in training," said Gia.

"Can't he give it a few days rest?"

"The triathlon is in eleven days. He can't slow down now."

"Well afterwards, then," Paul leaned over and poured another cup of tea.

They both sat for a moment in a comfortable silence.

"Are you still finding treasures?" Gia asked.

"I get out there before the refuse men and find all kinds of things. I'm working on furniture now. I came across a nice chair the other day. I'll fix the frame and Rose said she'd re-cover it. We take them to the auction house."

Rose and Paul had settled into a contented relationship. Rose had been on her own a long time after her husband had died. Both Rose and Gia's Aunt Grace had been friends with Paul for years. He did repairs and odd jobs for them and often took Rose to work when she cooked at the nursing home. In exchange, both ladies had treated Paul to home cooked meals.

"What was it you wanted to ask me, love?" said Paul.

What was it she wanted to ask him? Her mind was on other things. It was something to do with the shop. There were too many boxes . . .

"Shelves! I wondered if you could put some more shelves in the storage room. I need something that would be able to take boxes of plates and china. They can get heavy."

"I'll come down and take a look. Now I've lost my helper, I can't get as much done."

Paul was talking about Gia's cousin, Brian, who had found someone on a dating web site last year and taken off to Australia for three months to visit her.

"He'll be back," said Gia. "He always comes back."

That was another thing that had bothered Gia. Although she and Brian had both spent summers with Aunt Grace, they had lost touch for several years until Aunt Grace's death had brought them back together again. She didn't want to lose touch again. Would this woman he was seeing want to leave Australia if they got serious? Would Brian bring her here or would he want to move there?

"Your mum and dad look good," said Paul. "I don't see them out much."

That was because her mum didn't want to mix with normal folk like Rose and Paul. She had her sights set on the golf club. She couldn't see Rose and Paul stopping by the club house for cocktails with people who had hyphenated names.

"Mum's taken up golf. You know how she is?"

Paul shrugged. They all knew how her mother was. Most people reluctantly suffered her mother.

"I bet it's nice to have your mum and dad back though. Isn't it?"

"In some ways," said Gia.

Christmas had been eventful, as Rose put it, last year. She and David had only been married a few weeks and arrived home from their honeymoon a week before Christmas. Her mother had expected Gia to cook Christmas dinner and entertain them. Rose had wanted to cook dinner and have the whole family there. They opted to let Rose cook the turkey and Gia organized everyone else to take vegetables and pies over to her mother-in-law's house. Her mother had spoken unkindly about Gia during the meal and commented on her lack of cooking skills. Rose had said she thought Gia's cooking was just fine even though she herself had joked about Gia's lack of expertise in the kitchen. A frosty atmosphere had hung over the table for the remainder of the meal like a dark cloud that everyone expected would produce a clash of thunder at any moment.

"Holly and I are taking cooking classes up at the manor," she said.

Paul didn't look surprised that their conversation had changed. He knew better than to question how a woman's mind worked.

"That's nice, love," was all he said.

Gia stood and grabbed the rest of the tart and her tea mug and headed to the kitchen.

"I'll start looking out for scrap," said Paul. "No sense buying wood if we can help it. Lumber's expensive these days."

Rose had found a gem in Paul and she was glad the two of them were together.

"Everything will get sorted out. It always does," said Paul. "Have faith. By the way, Rose left a shepherd's pie for Collin. She said you were going to see him."

Holly was sitting on the doorstep when Gia closed the door to Rose and Paul's cottage.

"Before we go," said Holly when Gia crossed the driveway. "Are you feeling better? David said you were a bit queasy."

"Just some bug. A virus or something. Not much you can do with those except wait it out. I'm fine now," said Gia while opening the door to her home and placing the shepherd's pie on the counter.

"No point in taking a cooking class if you're not feeling well," continued Holly.

"I said, I'm fine," said Gia more abruptly than she'd planned to. "What are we making, anyway?"

"Monkfish curry."

That didn't sound appetizing and Gia felt her tummy gurgle.

Holly placed a tin, with a Victorian winter scene on the lid, next to the pie. She looked through the glass dish at the pie made with ground beef and carrots cooked in gravy and topped with mashed potatoes and garnished with cheese.

"Shepherd's pie is actually supposed to be made with lamb. Cottage pie is made with beef," said Holly.

Gia shrugged. "When did you become an expert?"

"I'm just saying," said Holly. "We've got an hour before the class, so hopefully Collin is at home and we can drop this off to him, offer our condolences and head on over to the manor. "Do you want me to drive," asked Holly.

The truth was that Gia's tummy continued to feel unstable and being behind the wheel seemed to help.

"No. We'll take my car."

They bundled everything in the back of Gia's green Volkswagen Golf and drove through Lowenna, up the hill with sand dunes piled high on the left, then turned down a lane which lead to a bluff, but they didn't continue on to the cliff, they turned right on to a fenced lane. The hamlet of Glasten was nestled among fields of barley and wheat which would soon be harvested. Sheep and goats wandered in the fields with a sharp incline and Gia spotted a few llamas that were kept for their wool. Her eye was immediately drawn to a Norman church with its square tower overlooking village cottages with slated roofs. As they drew closer, she saw that the cottages surrounded a village green, but ahead of them was the manor.

"Have you been up here before," Gia asked Holly when they pulled in front of the manor house.

"Not for years."

"How old do you think the manor house is?" Gia asked.

"Probably around the seventeenth century."

Gia eased herself from the car, but continued to look at the manor house. It wasn't the large, building she had expected. Built of Cornish stone, the tiled roof was uneven. Mullioned windows were narrow as was the arched door.

"The chimneys look like a wedding cake," said Holly.

Chimneys were lined up along the roof. Holly was right, they did look like the pillar supports of a tiered wedding cake.

But despite the colored stone, the house flowers brightened the exterior with pink hollyhocks, as high as she, blooming profusely in the garden. An old wooden wheelbarrow overflowed with pink and purple flowers. Ivy, begonias fuchsia

73

and forget-me-knots were tightly packed and cascaded over the rim.

Collin's farmhouse was a short walk from the manor.

A settee was partially leaning from the farmhouse window on the second floor. At the side of the cottage was a pine dresser, headboard and bed side tables.

"What's going on?" asked Gia.

"Looks like he's moving some stuff out," said Holly. "I always forget you didn't grow up around here. These old cob houses have very narrow stairs. Furniture has to be moved through the window or sometimes they have a trap door that you can drop large pieces through to the ground floor."

The settee was abruptly pulled back through the window opening

"I bet they'll try the trap door," said Holly. "Collin!" she called when she saw him walk out the front door.

"We bought you some food," said Gia. "We're so sorry about Meg."

Collin nodded. Gia thought he looked more angry than sad.

"Shall we put it in the kitchen?" offered Holly.

"Nice of you to think of me," he opened the door for them.

Above, a settee fell through a hole in the ceiling and into the arms of three men.

"I need to help them," Collin said and rushed over to ease the settee through the front door.

"Know anyone who needs some furniture?" asked one of the men. "We're helping Collin clean out Meg's room. He doesn't want to sell it, just wants someone to pick it up."

"I can't think of anyone," said Holly. "Do you Gia?"

"Paul might want it. He's been fixing up furniture. Let me give him a ring."

After she disconnected the call to Paul, she turned to Collin.

"Do you really not want any of it?" she nodded to a selection of bedroom furniture and a settee now lined up outside the cottage.

"I can't bear to look at it," he said. "I'll probably be moving soon anyway. Meg was the force behind trying to stop the sale of the manor farms. I don't have the energy for it."

"Paul Lanner said he'll come and pick it up."

"That's fine with me. Thanks for dinner," said Collin. "Look, I'd love to stop and chat, but you can see we're in the middle of getting everything out."

"That's okay," said Holly. "Stop by the William later. I'll be working if you want to chat."

"I may just do that," he said. "Thanks again. I'll bring your dishes back."

"What does Paul want with all that?" asked Holly when they walked back to the manor.

"He's been fixing up furniture and selling it at the auction house."

"Doesn't look very good," said Holly.

"Rose can recover it with good material and Paul can re-stain the furniture. I had no idea that's what they were doing. There's always a lot of activity in that shed in Rose and Paul's back garden."

"Perhaps that's what you and David need," said Holly. "A hobby you can do together."

Gia thought about this. They'd never needed a hobby. For the past couple of years they'd done everything together and it was Gia who had wanted David to take up something, to make new friends so that she didn't feel she lost her independence, but now she'd lost more than she'd bargained for.

A group of women stood outside the rear of the manor house.

"If you're here for the cooking class it's been cancelled," said Ruth Rundle, nodding toward a sign on the door.

Ruth leaned on her walker with both hands gripping it tightly.

Gia was surprised to see Ruth Rundle there.

"I'm Beryl," introduced one of the ladies. "This is Phyllis and Jennifer."

"You live here?" asked Gia, noticing that the only cars outside were hers and Ruth's.

"We live in the row of cottages, down by the stream," said Phyllis. "They used to be tied cottages for the farm workers."

"Tied?" asked Gia.

Beryl explained. "They were used by the workers on the farm. It would be tied to the job. If they left or were fired they lost their homes too. Often the tenants were given a plot of land to work for vegetables and to keep a cow or goat on. That way the landowner didn't have to pay as much in wages."

"That sounds harsh," said Gia.

"Better than working in the factories in London," said Holly.

And she was right. The factories during the industrial age had been no place to work with long hours, breathing stagnant air and dangerous conditions. The first strike in London was the match girls who in the 1800s worked in terrible conditions. Health problems resulted from the white phosphorous used on the matches and even young children worked fourteen hour days.

"And," added Beryl. "It's just a short walk to the beach from here. Not a bad life for a farmer. The wives often worked in the dairy and the children took time off from school to help during harvest time."

"But now you just rent the cottages?" asked Gia.

"It's not a bad rent and there aren't that many places you can live around here unless you have the money to buy a house," said Beryl. "Now people from the cities are wanting second homes and willing to pay an arm and a leg for them, there isn't much chance for locals to find somewhere to live."

"Meg was trying to get them to change their mind," said Phyllis. "But none of us has the enthusiasm to carry on after what happened to her. We're all wondering if she was killed because she stuck her nose in where it didn't belong. Why she was down on the beach at night was a mystery."

"So, you don't think she was taking Bailey for a walk?" asked Gia.

"No. He runs free around here. He's a friendly dog. He could have gone on his own along the pathway. That dog runs like the wind."

Gia noticed Ruth Rundle wasn't joining in the conversation. She turned and steered her walker toward her car. This time Beryl helped her in and put the walker in the back for her

Bailey ran to Gia and sat on her foot with his back to her. She rubbed his head and he thumped his tail enthusiastically on her leg.

"I'm glad he's okay at least," said Gia. "Poor thing."

"Have you thought?" asked Holly. "That if Meg didn't take Bailey with her he may have chased after her. Do you think she was meeting someone in Lowenna? The evenings are light until about ten o'clock so she would have been able to see if she walked along the pathway."

"I wonder," said Gia. "What Collin has to say about it."

"I'll ask him when he comes in for a drink. It's a bit too obvious questioning him now, don't you think?"

But when Paul went to pick up the furniture, Collin was gone, and all Paul could see through the window were a few boxes and Rose's casserole dish.

Chapter 8

"Moved out, just like that," said Rose when they met at Lowenna Antiques the following morning.

"I went with Paul to get the furniture," Rose continued. "Paul had a friend help him load it, but there was no sign of Collin. I did find my casserole dish in the kitchen. The front door was open."

"That was a bit odd," said Susan. "Why would he just take off like that?"

"Sounds suspicious to me," said Gia.

"Oh, everything sounds suspicious to you," said Rose. "He probably wanted to get away from all the memories. Those houses will probably be torn down once they start working on those holiday homes. I expect he's given up fighting for his family home now Meg's gone."

"Mum and dad have a brochure about a retirement community there," said Gia.

"Up at the manor?" asked Susan. "What about that lovely old house? It's been there for centuries."

"Surely they'll keep that and make it into a hotel or something. I don't know if the cottages will even be torn down. Holidaymakers from London and up north want to stay in an old cottage. Quaint they call it. Sandy Dunes Retirement Community, according to the map on the brochure mum and dad has, will be in one of the fields along with a golf course."

"Isn't Mrs. Gillard staying there?" asked Rose.

"I don't know if she really wants to," said Susan. "She says the house is getting too big for her. She didn't want to sell it though. She was considering renting it out."

This was something Beryl had told her yesterday.

"Don't the Gillards have any children?" asked Susan.

"I don't think so, but we're just surmising about what could happen," said Gia.

"That's what we're doing," agreed Susan. "Sumizering."

Rose shook her head when Susan mispronounced the word, but didn't correct her friend.

"We don't know that it's been sold yet and there seem to be plenty of people wanting to get their hands on it," said Gia.

"Mr. Gillard," Rose said to Susan, repeating what David had told them over Sunday dinner. "Left Glasten in his will to a trust."

"Why not his wife?" asked Susan. "That doesn't seem fair."

"The trust was supposed to protect everyone, his wife and the tenant farmers," said Gia.

"Lots of changes," said Rose.

"Did David like his dinner?" asked Susan. "I bet it was delicious."

After finding out the cooking class had been cancelled. Rose had invited Gia and Holly over to her house to show them how to make a steak and kidney pie, but Gia omitted the kidneys. They all had fun making the pastry and working together.

David had enjoyed the dinner she'd cooked which she had made supervised by his mother. Gia had been home in time to vacuum, clean the house and have the table set along with candles by the time he got home from work. They had taken the dogs for a walk along the cliffs, held hands and sat on the bench at the top of the cliffs listening to the waves beat against the rocks.

"He must have," said Rose. "You look a lot happier this morning. Been moping around like a wet rag lately, you have."

Gia had slept better than she had in weeks, and felt more invigorated this morning.

"I'm going to clean out the storage room and pack everything in boxes so that Paul can put up the shelves," said Gia making the most of her new found energy.

Gia began putting newspaper between the plates and packing each of them in a box. In the corner was a brown box that she didn't recognize.

"What's this?" she asked Susan when she came in to help.

"Collin Penhallow dropped it off. He said it was stuff his sister had collected and wanted to know if we could sell it for him. Rose felt sorry for him and said she'd see what she could do."

"Don't know where we're going to send the money if we sell it," said Rose from the doorway. "Now he's done a runner and no one knows where he is."

"What about Bailey?" asked Gia.

"Paul and me talked to Beryl while we were there. She has Bailey. She said she'd take him with her when she moves."

"So it looks like they're all giving up fighting for the farms then," said Susan. "What will happen to Glasten? It's such a lovely little hamlet."

But Rose and Gia just shook their heads.

"Lovely little hamlet," repeated Rose.

When Gia went home to take the dogs for a walk, Paul was in the back garden pulling the covering off the settee they had picked up from Collin's cottage. The pink tapestry material was faded and threadbare in places.

"Do you think it's worth saving?" asked Gia.

"Once Rose has got new material, you'll never know it looked like this," said Paul who had turned it over to look at the structure of the bottom. "We're thinking of opening a little shop in Truro. It's too touristy here for something like furniture."

Paul and Rose were going to Truro too? What was the matter with everyone?

"You're not thinking of moving are you?" she asked.

"No. I'll run the shop. It won't be such heavy work as I've been having to do lately."

When Gia helped him to turn the settee upright the cushions fell off and there was a large burgundy stain on one of the seats.

"What's that?" asked Paul. "I hope it hasn't gone all the way through to the padding. Could it be red wine?"

Gia didn't speak for a moment, but stared at the stain and imagined the night it seeped into the material. She gave an involuntary shudder.

"It looks like blood," said Gia. "I think we need to call Detective Inspector Barrett."

She began punching in numbers on her phone before Paul could argue.

After the detective left, taking the seat cushion with him, Gia hooked on the dogs' leashes and walked down the hill to the King William.

Holly joined her outside. She put a bowl of fresh water by the dogs and another by the door to the pub. Dogs were as much part of the pub's customers as were their masters. She sat across from Gia on the wooden bench.

"On the settee?" asked Holly after Gia explained what they had found. "So it was Collin, then."

"Not necessarily. We don't know if it was her blood, but if it was, it could have been someone else who killed her. It just means she was injured in her own room. The settee was upstairs wasn't it?"

"I think," said Holly. "that she used the second floor and he used the ground floor. Except the kitchen that is. They shared that."

"I bet the police are searching the cottage for whatever it was that killed her," said Gia. "What we need to find out is who's in charge of that development company that's trying to buy the manor. If one of them was up at the house on Thursday evening then they could well be on the list of suspects."

"Whose list? Yours or the police?" asked Holly with a raise of her well defined eyebrow.

"What do you mean by that?" asked Gia.

"Well, you're always stirring everything up."

"Why are you being so defensive? I'm not accusing you of anything. Wait a minute . . ." Gia paused and looked closely at Holly. "What *is* Maximo doing here?"

Holly looked away.

"He's involved isn't he?"

"His family is interested in buying land around here," said Holly.

"Where was he on Thursday?" asked Gia. "Thursday evening."

"We were together, but I don't see him every day. Come on, Gia you're taking this too far."

Holly stood abruptly, but left Gia wondering if the charming Maximo had something to do with Meg's death.

She pushed her drink away. She didn't feel like drinking or eating anything. Should she tell Detective Inspector Barrett? But what would she tell him? She had suspicions only, and if she was wrong Holly would be more than angry with her than she already was.

Gia decided to wait to talk to the detective until she did some more investigating.

Back at Lowenna Antiques, Gia continued boxing up the plates and ornaments from the storage room. Perhaps Paul would have some time to put in the shelves for them.

Susan hovered in the doorway reminding Gia of Tigger from her childhood Winnie the Pooh books. The tiny woman bounced on her trainers.

"I think he's the one," Susan finally said as if her little chest with burst.

"Who? What?" asked Gia, confused.

"Percy Legg." Susan blushed.

Percy did it, thought Gia. Percy killed Meg?

"He knew Meg Penhallow?" Gia asked.

Susan's face dropped. She frowned. "What do you mean?"

Gia realized she was the only one thinking about murder. Susan had something else on her mind.

"I think he's going to ask me to marry him," said Susan.

"But I thought you didn't want to get married. You've always said you just wanted to have some fun."

"That was before I met him. Gia, he's like the other part of me. Ping and pong. It's Japanese for people who complement each other."

"Do you mean yin and yang? I think it's Chinese."

"Yes, That's it. I read about it on boogle. Together we are whole," said Susan with feeling.

She'd never seen Susan this bad over someone and there had been plenty of boyfriends through the years. Rose was going to have something to say about this and it wouldn't be good. Rose felt the need to protect everyone, including herself and had held Paul at a distance for years until finally agreeing to marry him. She'd remind Rose of that when she started telling Susan she didn't want her to get her heart broken.

"I think I'm in love," said Susan and put her hand over her heart. "Amore."

Before Gia could comment that amore was Italian and not French that Susan had purported to be learning, she stopped. It wasn't only Susan's head that was spinning. Gia leaned against the shelf. Too much thinking, too much worrying and too many things bouncing around in her head. Gia steadied herself.

"Are you all right?" asked Susan and gripped Gia's arm. "Here. Come and sit down."

Susan guided Gia toward the table and pulled out a chair. Gia slumped into it.

"I just felt a bit dizzy," said Gia. She patted Susan's hand. "I'm pleased for you. That's exciting news."

Susan gave Gia a glass of water, pulled out another chair and sat facing her.

"Him and John are going out to see if they can catch another tuna," said Susan.

"They are. Why?"

Because John says they should get it checked in London to see if they can get commercial fishing license for it. If there are tuna around here, it would make a big difference now that some of the fish are getting depleted.

"In John's boat?" Gia asked.

"No. They're taking the Mermaid."

But Gia didn't voice her concerns or her fears. Neither John Trewellyn nor Percy Legg were young men. Hauling a fish the size of a small car would not be an easy task.

It wasn't long before Ruth Rundle hobbled back into the shop.

"We had a delivery yesterday," said Gia. "Susan, could you check and see if Mrs. Rundle's order has arrived?"

"Was there something else we could help you with?" asked Gia more cheerily than she felt.

"Your stuff is too expensive," said Ruth. "I wouldn't have bought this except I want to keep in with the lady of the manor. I'm on disability living allowance, you know."

Yes, they all knew. Ruth wasn't doing too badly for someone who had retired early. Then Gia felt badly for thinking that way. If the woman was in pain, it wasn't a good way to get out of working, but she had her doubts that this was the case.

Rose shook her rain coat at the front door and removed a plastic hat.

"Coming down cats and dogs," she said.

"I didn't hear it," said Susan peering out the window.

The wind changed direction and rain beat on to the window.

They all turned to Ruth.

"No point in you leaving, yet," Rose said to her.

"Susan, put the kettle on will you and we'll have a nice cuppa." Rose put her coat and hat on a coat stand. "This will pass in no time."

But Susan stood by the window and stared.

"What's wrong with you?" asked Rose.

"John and Percy are out fishing," said Susan.

"Well, I hate to state the obvious, but they are fishermen," said Rose. "I have an idea. Why don't you stand and stare out the window and I'll go and put the kettle on," said Rose with a sarcastic note to her voice.

"Fine mess that settee was," said Rose to Gia and made no attempt to move toward the kitchenette.

"Settee," asked Ruth.

Gia didn't want to get into the intricacies of Paul and Rose's new found hobby, nor did she want to discuss what they had found, which she didn't think Paul had shared with Rose.

"Come and sit over here Mrs. Rundle," Gia said, pulling out a chair. "Make yourself comfortable and I'll get the biscuit tin and put the kettle on."

Rose hadn't noticed that Gia specified biscuit tin and hopefully they wouldn't be catering to Mrs. Rundle with the special plate and best cups and saucers. She had been mayor for heaven's sake not the Queen of England and she hadn't even been mayor of Lowenna.

"Susan!" said Rose. "You're not going to let Gia make the tea are you?"

Apparently that was the worst thing that could happen in Lowenna Antiques. Gia never made the tea strong enough, put in too much milk and didn't let it brew the required length of time.

"If you put the tea in first you would know how much milk to add," said Gia in her own defense. "How do you know how strong the tea is? It's silly to put the milk in first."

"Bone china," said Susan who had reluctantly turned from the window.

"We don't have bone china," said Rose.

Ruth was sorting through the biscuits in the tin and slipping one or two in her pocket. Gia made a mental note not to touch any of the biscuits that had been thoroughly handled.

"It's when everyone used bone china," said Susan.

"We never did," added Rose. "Always good old sturdy stuff, that didn't break at the drop of a pin, for us."

"If . . . ," said Susan with a sigh. ". . . you pour in hot water first, it cracks the cup. That's why the nobility started putting the milk in before pouring the tea."

"So," said Gia. "We *can* put the tea in first. We don't use bone china so it won't crack."

"You're not making the tea," said Rose with feeling. "And we *will* make it properly."

Ruth continued to move biscuits around with her finger tips as if expecting another layer to appear.

"You don't have any chocolate digestives do you?" Ruth asked.

"We may have," Susan said. "I'll just go and look."

There wasn't any reason Gia should dislike Ruth Rundle, but she did. There was something about her. The cunning way she looked at people as if seeing what she could get away with. She seemed to round her back as if trying to make herself smaller, or perhaps appear older, but Gia judged Ruth to be taller than she. Gia had a feeling Ruth Rundle was not an honest person.

Susan neither went to look for the digestive biscuits nor made the tea. She hadn't left the spot she'd been standing in for several minutes and returned her gaze to the window.

"Do you think they'll be all right? Percy and John. Do you think their boat is safe?"

"Of course it is," said Rose with a hint of annoyance. "Why wouldn't they be? They've been in storms before and that son of Percy's is a good navigator."

86

"He didn't go with them," said Susan, her face full of fear.

"Perhaps they haven't left. Wouldn't they have checked the forecast?" asked Gia.

"I saw them leave this morning," said Susan.

Rose turned to Susan. "They'll be fine, love. They didn't get to this age without knowing what they're doing, did they? Go and get those biscuits for Mrs. Rundle and we'll sit down and have a nice cup of tea."

Gia had cleaned out the electric kettle, removing some of the calcium build up which only she noticed as it blended with the milk in their cups and she took hers without any milk.

"That was a downpour," said Paul when he rushed into the shop, and after Gia had made the tea despite continued protests from Rose. "Good, you've got the kettle on," he said.

"Pull up a chair, Paul," said Gia.

"I'll wait a bit until I get the shelves and tools out of the truck. "It's still drizzling a bit."

Gia hoped Ruth would be leaving soon. She wanted to talk to Paul about the settee and didn't want Ruth overhearing. She reminded Gia of a weasel.

Rose also was acting as if she wanted Ruth to leave. The bowing that Rose had done a few days ago had been replaced by her usual brusqueness.

"Here's your umbrella," she said and thrust it into the hands of Ruth who had barely finished drinking her tea.

She stood and wobbled a little before Susan helped her with her walker and between them they moved to the door. Susan hooked the umbrella on to the walker and helped her over the threshold.

"Rose, you were a little rude," said Susan from the doorway.

"She was pinching our biscuits," said Rose. "That's just not done."

So that was all it took for Rose to change her opinion of someone. Gia had to admit, it was a bit rude pocketing biscuits.

"Susan!" said Rose. "Put the wood in the hole will you? It's chilly in here and standing there with the door open isn't helping."

But Gia watched Susan move this way and that, leaning to her left and then her right trying to get a good view of the harbor. With a dejected expression, she gently closed the door, but it soon opened again.

"They're all right," said Iris Trewellyn when she burst into the shop.

"Who's all right?" asked Rose.

"The men."

Rose was still puzzled, but Susan's eyes lit up.

"Percy and John?" asked Susan.

"Yes. John radioed," said Iris. "They'll be back soon."

"Any tuna sightings?" asked Susan.

Rose stood with her hands on hips about to verbalize that her little friend had lost her mind, but lowered them and asked Iris if she would like a cup of tea.

"I must get back to the shop, but I knew Susan would be worried. John didn't say if they had seen or caught any tuna," she added.

"You'll be quoting weather forecasts next," said Rose when Iris closed the door.

Paul returned and began hammering and drilling in the storage room.

"I'll take Paul a cup of tea," said Gia and watched both women for their expression.

When neither of them commented, she backed toward the kitchen, refilled the tea pot and poured what she thought was an acceptable cup of tea.

"What did Detective Inspector Barrett say?" she whispered to Paul.

"He brought a couple of blokes with him. They cut the material off the settee and told me not to do anything until they had it tested."

"And you haven't told Rose?" she asked quietly.

"No. Don't want her to get in a tizzy about it. We'll let her know in due course."

"I'll call him later and see what he says," said Gia.

She put the tea cup on the shelf and left Paul gazing into it as if reading tea leaves.

"Mrs. Rundle forgot her plate and saucer," said Susan and picked up the wrapped package on the counter.

"She'll be back, then," said Rose. "Don't get out the biscuit tin if she comes again."

"I think that's the Mermaid," said Gia when she looked out the window. "They're just coming into the harbor."

But Susan hadn't heard her, the bell tinkled, the door slammed and Susan was running as fast as her little feet could go across the car park and along the harbor wall.

"Got it bad this time," said Rose with a sigh that came from deep within her cavity.

Gia didn't trust herself to speak, but nodded.

"I've never seen her like this," added Rose. "Most of the time she's away with the fairies, but this time it's worse."

"She really likes Percy," said Gia.

"Like! She's head over heels."

And then Rose said something that surprised Gia.

"This one may work out," said Rose.

"You don't think she'll get her heart broken?" asked Gia.

"The others were fly-by-nights. Percy is a good man. He's lived in the village for years. Susan could do a lot worse. Susan deserves a little bit of happiness. All those years she looked after her parents. That dolt ran off to Australia and left her. Bob the biker went back to Canada and then there was that doctor. We all knew that couldn't come to any good. He had one foot in the grave. But Percy – he's different."

There wasn't much Gia could say to this. Rose was right and she didn't think Susan had considered any of these boyfriends seriously. Except perhaps the doctor. That was definitely a shock.

"We won't have another winter wedding, though," said Rose. "Yours was a disaster. Better to wait for the spring."

Gia didn't consider her wedding a disaster. She had to agree it hadn't gone as planned, but being snowed in with her closest friends wasn't a bad way to get married. Of course there were a few mishaps, but no one had been injured.

"No tuna," said Susan breathlessly when she returned. "They're mooring now. If you don't mind, I'd like to go home for a bit and then Percy's taking me out to dinner. I need to stop by the chemist first."

Susan didn't wait for either of them to respond. She'd grabbed a quilted bag that she kept everything in that didn't fit in her apron pocket and headed to the door. There was no mistaking the smile and wave she gave when she left.

"Got it bad, she has," repeated Rose. "I wonder why she wanted to go to the chemist," she dismissed the thought with a shrug of her shoulders. "Now, let's go and look at those shelves."

Beryl came in Lowenna Antiques later with Bailey.

"While you were in Collin's did you see anything that Meg left behind?" asked Beryl.

"What kind of anything?" Gia wanted to know.

"As you know, she'd been trying to stop them selling the tenant farms and she must have found something out."

"I thought you were resigned to moving?" said Gia.

"Well, we thought we'd give it one more chance. That is, if we can find something. Meg had a notebook with everything she'd been doing in it."

Gia thought for a moment.

"There were a lot of papers around, but I think Collin took everything. Do you want me to come with you to look?"

"Don't get involved," said Rose.

"I'm just going to look. No harm in looking," said Gia.

As she said it, she felt disloyal. Her mum was excited about a retirement community, but was it fair that people were moved from their homes so that others could indulge themselves? As she said, there was no harm in looking. What the tenants did with the information was another matter.

"Let's go," said Gia.

She shrugged in to her jacket and left Rose in the shop alone.

Chapter 9

Bailey rested his head on Gia's shoulder while she drove and drool fell from his open mouth. She reached behind and scratched his head.

"How's he doing?" she asked Beryl.

"He keeps going back to the cottage like he's looking for Meg and Collin."

When they reached the cottage, Gia tried the front door – it was locked.

The two of them walked around to the back and found the handle turned easily.

"Meg used the upstairs," said Beryl as both of them walked up the narrow staircase toward the room at the front of the house.

Beneath the window was a desk with papers strewn everywhere.

"Looks like Collin left in a hurry," said Gia.

"He didn't tell anyone he was going," said Beryl. "I'm surprised he gave up so easily. This house has been in his family for generations."

"Unless he killed his sister," said Gia. "It may have been an accident," she added.

She thought of the red stain on the settee. Could Meg have hit her head?

"Then why . . . ?" asked Beryl ". . . was she found in the car park. Collin wouldn't have dumped his sister out in the open like that."

"It had to be someone who was strong enough to carry her," said Gia.

"So you think she was killed here?" asked Beryl.

But Gia felt she'd said more than she intended and she shrugged.

"I don't know. Let's start looking for that notebook."

They hadn't looked for more than a few minutes before Bailey started barking and when Gia looked out the window there was the unmistakable black Ford Escort that Detective Inspector Barrett drove.

"Darn. We'd better get out of here," said Beryl grabbing, a pile of papers.

While the detective climbed from the car, Beryl and Gia headed to the top of the stairs with Bailey at their heels and when Gia turned, Bailey had a notebook in his mouth. She took it, wiped the slobber from the book on the side of her leg and without Beryl noticing, popped it into her pocket.

Before the detective could open the door, the two of them had run through the garden that was bordered with bushes, and were on their way to Beryl's house. Gia glanced over her shoulder as the detective opened the back door.

"Too bad we didn't find anything," said Beryl when she put the copper kettle on to the stove.

"Too bad," echoed Gia feeling her pocket for the book.

"Do you want to wait here for a bit?" asked Beryl.

"Probably until the detective leaves," said Gia.

She looked around the small cottage with its wooden beams and uneven walls. The ceilings were low, the builders not expecting future generations to be taller.

"It's cool in here," said Gia.

"The cob walls are pretty thick. They used mud and straw for the walls and then filled in between with rubble and rocks."

The kitchen faced the back of the house and Gia gazed at the garden. She hadn't expected anything quite so manicured.

The grass was a kidney shape with borders of pink hollyhocks, red roses, and blue delphiniums. At the end of the garden was an arbor with pale yellow climbing roses.

"Your garden is beautiful," said Gia.

"It took us a long time to get it how we want it," said Beryl. "We started by double digging."

"What does that mean?"

"You dig a trench and leave the soil in a heap, then next to the trench you dig down about eight to twelve inches and fill it in with the soil from the first trench. You continue like that for the whole garden. It breaks up the soil, moves the nutrients to the top where young plants need it, and gets rid of the weeds because you pull those out as you go along. It takes a long time, but it's worth it."

"You're not going to want to leave are you?" asked Gia.

She felt again in her pocket for the notebook, wondering if she should divulge to Beryl what she found. After all, that had been what the two of them were looking for. But she convinced herself that it would be better if she viewed the notebook first. She was an uninterested party. But was she? Her mother wanted the land sold so that her parents could move into a comfortable retirement community where they could play golf and mingle with others from that community. No matter what her mother wanted, it just wasn't right that these people who had taken care of the land should have to leave, but she did feel a twinge of guilt going against what her mother wanted and trying to help the manor tenants.

"I may not have a choice," said Beryl.

"Where will you go?" asked Gia.

"I don't know. I have some savings so I might be able to look into buying something, but it's all so expensive now. If I had known I was going to have to leave my home, I would have bought something else years ago before all the prices went sky high. It was supposed to be tenancy for life. We pay our rent to the trust and they were instructed to use the rent to maintain the land just like Mr. Gillard wanted."

"And what about that lovely chapel?" asked Gia.

"They'll turn that into a house probably. No one has any use for those little chapels any more. Gone are the days when the village worshipped together."

Gia thought of the place where she had eaten dinner with David the other night. That had also once been a local chapel where people from the village worshipped together and it was now a restaurant. Were times changing for the better? She didn't think so.

"Looks like he's leaving, said Beryl when she peered out the living room window. We can get going if you've finished your tea."

They returned to Lowenna Antiques and Gia found Rose reading a magazine while she knitted squares. Gia watched Rose feel for the stitches with her fingers and continue knitting along the row without looking at her work.

"Took your time," said Rose. "Did you find anything?"

Gia pulled out the notebook, the black leather scuffed and the corners torn.

"I found this," Gia said.

"Well, let's have a look, then," said Rose, putting her knitting on the table.

Gia opened the first page, then closed the book.

"It's like a diary. I'm not sure we should be looking."

"Can't do any harm now can it, love?" Rose said.

"Suppose not."

She opened the book again, thinking of Meg when she had scribbled her thoughts into the book.

Gia skipped over where Meg talked of her fiancé, her thoughts for their life together and it wasn't too many pages later that Meg had penned that each of the tenants had received a letter telling them that their tenancy would be coming to an end. Gia went behind the counter and found a note pad and began making notes of dates.

It was a month ago that they had received notice. But that seemed premature as no one seemed sure that the manor farms could actually be sold at that time. They still didn't know. What she needed was a copy of Mr. Gillard's will. That way she could take it to Mr. Alderton, the solicitor, and see if what the college was doing was legitimate. But Meg may have already sought the advice of a solicitor. She read on.

"What does it say," asked Rose as she began to cast off stitches to a crimson red square.

"Nothing much. The tenants received notice that their farms were being sold."

"That shouldn't be allowed," said Rose. "Can't you do something?"

That caught Gia by surprise because just this morning Rose was telling her it was none of her business.

"I think Ruth Rundle is involved in this," said Rose.

"How could she?" asked Gia. "She doesn't have anything to do with the manor."

"I used to like the woman, but there's something going on with her. She was acting very shifty like she knew something she didn't want us to find out."

Gia still felt that Meg's murder and the sale of the manor farms were connected, but she could be wrong.

Thoughts swirled through Gia's mind. How could she get her hands on a copy of the will?

For a few moments neither of them spoke. Rose continued reading her ladies' magazine, and Gia turned pages of The Westerner newspaper. A small article on page three caught her attention. It was about the tenant farms. Reporters could find out all kinds of information. She made a note of the byline and then looked at the front of the newspaper for a phone number.

"Anything else in the diary?" asked Rose.

Before the two ladies could consider the diary further, Susan burst into the shop and they instantly knew what she had bought at the chemist. Susan's hair was bright red!

"Could we meet for coffee?" asked Gia when she talked to the reporter.

She wanted to speak face to face.

"How about eleven tomorrow morning?"

They agreed to meet at a pub in Truro and Gia pocketed her phone.

After the initial shock of Susan's hair, Gia had to admit that it brightened up her face and gave her some color. It was then she realized that Susan was also wearing makeup. It was tastefully done and looked natural.

"The girl at the chemist said she would experiment a bit," said Susan and admired herself in the mirror. "Percy's taking me out to dinner tonight."

"You've been eating out a lot. Aren't you going to make him a home cooked meal?" asked Rose who didn't see the point of eating in a restaurant when there was perfectly good food at home.

"He's been to my house on more than one occasion," said Susan and blushed.

"I see," said Rose although she didn't at all.

After they closed the shop, Paul took Rose home, and Susan left to get ready for her dinner with Percy. Gia pocketed the diary and walked across the beach and along the cliff path.

What had happened to make her world spin out of control? Susan was not only thinking of marriage, but had dyed her hair red for heaven's sake. Paul was looking for a shop in Truro. Would Rose want to give up Lowenna Antiques and help him in the shop? Her mum and dad had their sights set on a retirement community, which was something she never thought would be uttered from her mother's mouth, and David – well David was caught up in the whole triathlon thing and who knew if they would ever get back to normal again. Then there was Holly.

She'd been happy at the pub for years, why did she now want to go off to Truro? Not that it was far, only ten miles, but still.

Gia sat on a bench watching the white caps. Seagulls fought against the wind. A rock jutted from the headland with an arch looking like an open window. Out to sea, puffins inhabited an island. Fishing boats came and went, holiday charter boats left the harbor for an evening of fishing and in the distance tanker ships hugged the horizon. She saw the gorse bush rustle. The yellow flowered prickly plant moved sharply and then she heard a soft growling sound and Bailey bounded from the bush, jumped on to the bench next to her and slumped his head onto her lap.

"Where did you come from?" she asked him and he slapped his tail against the bench.

She looked to her right and then her left, but couldn't see Beryl anywhere.

It was then she realized, she'd walked so far along the coast that the manor house and farms were probably behind her and just over the sand dune.

This explained how Bailey had got to the beach. But what about Meg? If that was her blood on the settee then she would hardly have walked down the sand dunes and along the cliff road at night, or had it happened early in the morning? Regardless, with that amount of blood lost, she would have been in no state to walk anywhere.

She opened her phone and dialed Detective Inspector Barrett's number.

"Anything new on Meg Penhallow's case?" she asked without preamble.

"Miss . . . Mrs. Penrose . . . Gia," he stuttered. "You know I can't divulge anything about an ongoing case. Where are you?" he asked.

"I'm on the cliff pathway," said Gia. "Bailey's with me."

"Collin Penhallow's dog?"

"Yes. I don't think Meg had been taking him for a walk that morning."

"She died Thursday evening," said the detective. "The M.E. confirmed the time of death."

"Whenever it was, I think Bailey ran along this path to find her."

"Interesting thoughts," said the detective. "She wasn't killed where we found her."

"The blood on the settee was hers?" asked Gia.

"Looks that way."

Despite Detective Inspector Barrett's reluctance to tell her anything, he was giving her a lot of information.

We have an APW . . . an all points warning out for Collin Penhallow. Looks like Meg was killed in the cottage and left in the car park."

"But how would he have got her there? He only has a motor bike."

"How can you run a farm with just a motor bike?"

"He had people helping him."

"Then maybe he had an accomplice."

This widened the net. Who would have helped him dispose of Meg's body?

"They were close," said Gia. "Collin and his sister cared for each other."

"So I heard."

"He wouldn't have just left her there. You don't do that to someone you care about."

They each agreed to keep the other informed if they found anything new, but Gia knew that neither of them would adhere to that promise.

Bailey removed his head and she watched him climb the steep embankment of the sand dunes and his tail wagged until it was obliterated by tufts of tall grass that had spurted up in the sand. And then he was gone.

She was back to considering the developers of Sandy Dunes Retirement Community as a suspect. Was that the reason Max had arrived in the West Country?

Chapter 10

"Are you going to the auction today?" Rose asked, turning to Gia. "Paul went to look yesterday and he said there's some Royal Worcester china that we might be interested in."

"I'll be in Truro this morning anyway," said Gia. "I'll go and see if there's anything that might be worth bidding on."

"Why?" asked Susan.

"Because if it's incomplete sets we can sell it for replacements."

"No," said Susan. "Why are you going to Truro?"

Gia paused. What did she want to divulge? Did she want to tell them she was meeting a reporter? If anything came out in the newspaper they didn't like, she was sure to be blamed and Rose and Susan talked a lot. They talked to anyone who walked through the door of Lowenna Antiques without thinking about what *news* they were spreading.

"Probably meeting David for lunch," offered Rose and Gia didn't correct her.

Music blared from the radio. Susan swished her feather duster in between candles, ornaments, and plates displayed on stands, thrusting it in the air occasionally during the louder notes of Band on the Run. Paul McCartney was one of Susan's favorites.

Gia waved to Rose and closed the door behind her.

Following the road parallel to the river, Gia passed a row of terraced cottages and then came across the thatched roofed pub where Philip Hodges had suggested they meet. It had windows trimmed with dark wood and colorful hanging baskets brightened the white walls with pink fuchsia, red geraniums and purple lobelia cascading from them.

She found a seat outside on the small patio where, on the other side of the road, was the river.

"Did you know that thousands of American troops were stationed downstream not far from here?" asked the reporter and pulled out a wooden chair.

They both looked out toward the river.

"Here?" asked Gia. "In Cornwall?"

"In preparation for D-Day. Eisenhower came to speak to them before they left to cross over to France."

"Philip Hodges," he said and Gia shook his outstretched hand.

"I saw your article in the Westerner," said Gia. "The one about the local hamlets and villages. You mentioned Glasten."

"I believe that isn't the last we've heard of that small village." said the reporter, placing a portfolio overflowing with paper on to the seat next to him. "It's sure to blow up into a bigger story, may even end up being picked up by newspapers in other counties. A small hamlet taken over by big business. Tenants turfed out in the street. People still want to believe in old world charm and they hate to think of a time when English villages and hamlets are no more. Even if they themselves want to stay in their houses in the city, it's nice to know villages still exist somewhere. Postcards with all the Cornish harbors and views like this one. . ." He nodded toward the river. ". . . will one day be collector's items."

"No one sends postcards anymore," said Gia, knowing their post card stand at Lowenna Antiques was merely a dust collector. "Anyone on holiday simply posts their pictures on Facebook."

"Exactly my point," said Philip Hodges.

"You're not from here are you?" asked Gia, noting his strong midland accent.

He smiled and his eyes, that had at first seemed squinted, opened wider behind square bronze trimmed glasses. His short hair was an auburn color and he had a neatly trimmed beard a shade lighter. Gia wondered how David would look with a beard.

"Birmingham," he said. "I came down here camping with some lads. We pitched our tent in a farmer's field. Not a place unlike the farms around Glasten."

"So, you have a personal interest too?" asked Gia.

"You could say that. The small villages and hamlets are what attracted me to Cornwall. But why is this something you're involved in?"

"Off the record?"

He shrugged. "You can't tell a reporter something and expect it to be off the record."

"Let me put it this way, then. Please don't use my name or use anything that would point to me."

"Fair enough."

"You heard about the woman who was found murdered in the car park in Lowenna?" Gia asked.

"I don't do crime," said the reporter. "That's not my patch."

"I think it's connected to the village. To Glasten."

"How so?"

"She was fighting for the village. Trying to stop it from being sold. Meg Penhallow had a petition going. She was very vocal about what was going on. I'm surprised you didn't interview her."

"I talked to a lot of people. I had enough to write a story about Cornish hamlets disappearing to make room for second homes and holidaymakers. What Meg Penhallow was doing seems harmless stuff."

"But whoever buys the property won't want bad press will they?"

"You have a point."

"What can you tell me about the estate?" asked Gia. "All I know is that Mr. Gillard left a will that said the manor and land had to remain intact and continue to be rented to the tenants after his demise."

"That isn't exactly what happened."

He ordered a lager for each of them and a cheese and tomato sandwich for himself. Gia declined anything to eat.

"The owner of the manor estate, Mr. Gillard, died in the late fifties and you're right he did want to keep the estate in tact so he set up a trust. He chose the college he attended in Hampshire to be the trustee."

"But they're two hundred miles away. How could they oversee anything from Hampshire?"

"Mr. Gillard felt the institution would be the best option as a trustee to take care of his wishes. It wasn't unusual. There are a lot of colleges that own land and receive rent. You may remember a few years ago a television program called Michael Wood's story of England."

Gia shook her head. It wasn't something she remembered.

"Michael Wood encouraged the residents of a village in Leicestershire to excavate a small patch in each of their back gardens. He was able to trace the history of the village by what they uncovered going back to Roman occupation of Britain," said the reporter.

"What does that have to do with Glasten?" asked Gia.

"As part of his research he uncovered documents from a college who had originally bought the estate in the thirteenth century. It wasn't uncommon for colleges to own hamlets and villages. Mr. Gillard was probably hoping for the same arrangement for Glasten. I expect he considered it safer to select a college as a trustee than an individual person."

"So, why is the college trying to sell the estate which is blatantly against Mr. Gillard's wishes?" Gia wanted to know.

"It's worked out fine for both the tenants and Mrs. Gillard for all these years. It was when the college appointed a new director that the situation changed. He saw an opportunity to sell the hamlet when he was contacted by a wind turbine group. Being close to the dunes, it would be a prime place to put in turbines."

"But surely, if they are holding the land in trust, the college should continue to abide by Mr. Gillard's wishes?" asked Gia.

"You would think so. But what they did was open a can of worms. The Charity Commission got involved."

"Why the Charity Commission?" asked Gian even more confused.

"The college is set up as a charity. The Commission declared that the college didn't meet the criteria for charities. It got complicated and the college was told they could no longer hold it as a trust."

"So who will be the trustee?" Gia frowned, trying to assimilate what she was hearing.

"As I said, it's complicated. Obviously the locals don't want to lose their tenancy. Whatever happens it will be a battle."

Philip Hodges gave Gia his business card in case she wanted to share any information that he may be able to use in future articles and Gia let him know he could always reach her at Lowenna Antiques.

From the corner of her eye, she saw Mrs. Jones and her sister Maisie leave the pub and cross the road toward a parked car. She watched them drive away and was relieved she didn't have to talk to either of them. Mrs. Jones could depress even Father Christmas.

"I'm in Truro," said Gia when she called David later that morning. "Can we have lunch?"

"Sounds serious," said David.

"We don't ever see each other," said Gia.

"You wake up next to me every morning," said David and she could hear laughter in his voice.

That was true. What she meant to say was they hardly ever speak, but David would consider *hello* and *goodbye* speaking. But even he had to agree that conversation between the two of them seemed to happen rarely these days.

"How about in the park? I'll bring sandwiches," Gia suggested.

She'd come to a decision and wanted to talk to David. There was too much going on in their lives. Having the stomach bug made her think twice about getting pregnant. They had plenty of time. The queasiness she'd felt was probably like morning sickness and she simply didn't have time to get sick every morning. Rose and Susan wouldn't be able to run the shop without her.

David agreed to meet her in an hour at Victoria Gardens.

She stopped at the bakery where smells of freshly baked bread filled her nostrils and made her mouth water. Buying crusty rolls filled with cheese and creamy coleslaw, Gia grabbed two bottles one of water and the other Pepsi that she knew David liked.

In the center of the gardens, the pathway circled a fountain profusely bordered with begonias and anchored by a wrought iron bandstand decorated with bronze metal sunbeams set in the railing. Four benches faced the fountain and flower beds filled with marigolds, lilies and petunias were neatly placed along the green.

"This is nice," said David refusing the drink and instead drinking out of a water container he'd brought with him.

When had that happened? He always liked Pepsi.

"I sense there's something you want to say," he said while he unwrapped his sandwich.

"I don't want children," said Gia without preamble.

David lowered his sandwich and swallowed slowly the bread that was in his mouth.

"What brought this on?" he asked.

"I don't want to be sick. I don't want to be as big as a house."

"I can't help you out there," said David with a hesitant laugh.

Gia didn't smile.

A red ball rolled down the grassy incline and David stopped it with his foot, picked it up and threw the ball to a boy who had been following its path.

She reached for David's hand and he gripped hers tightly. She could see it pained him.

"I don't mean ever. Just not now. Perhaps next year," she said hopefully.

"No one is ever ready for children, Gia," said David.

A toddler ran past them, followed by his mother who was holding a tiny baby. She hitched the baby on to her hip and used the other hand to ease the toddler away from the water filled fountain.

"I'm scared," Gia admitted.

"Look. We'll wait and talk about it again in a few months. We've been married less than a year. There's no harm in waiting."

David was being kind, but she could see it bothered him.

"Come here," he said.

David put his sandwich on the bench and held out his arm which she snuggled into. Her sobs were soft at first, but then grew louder and he hugged her tightly until her body stopped shaking.

"Let's finish our lunch and have a walk in the park. It's a lovely day."

And it was a lovely day. Relieved of her burden, Gia felt her shoulders loosen, her body felt lighter. David turned to reach for his sandwich, but a squirrel had already spotted it and after pushing it from the bench, was dragging it across the grass.

They both laughed and so did the children watching.

At the auction that afternoon, she saw Paul who had several pieces of furniture for sale. A set of dining chairs, the seat of which Rose had recovered with paisley material. Paul had refinished and stained the wood. There were two small tables.

"This was all dumped outside Collin Penhallow's place," said Paul. "It would have been a shame to let it all go to waste. Good furniture it is. Solid."

And it was nice furniture and Paul and Rose had done a great job at fixing it up.

"I've found a little shop," said Paul. "I think it will work a treat for selling some of the stuff we have in the shed."

Gia didn't know what to say. She still worried that Rose would want to give up working at Lowenna Antiques. With the three of them it meant they could each have the time off they wanted. And then if Susan got married would she still want to continue working there? It could be the end of the little business they'd built up, but there was always their web site. Gia could spend more time getting that up to date and selling replacement dishes through mail order. It would work out and she just had to adjust to whatever changes came their way. After talking to David, she felt she could handle anything. Once they, or she, had decided to wait for a while to have children, it was a big weight off her mind.

"I talked to Rose," said Paul. "She doesn't mean any harm, love. She's just excited."

"About that," said Gia. "We've decided to wait. It just isn't a good time for us."

"I doubt it is ever a good time, but what do I know? I was a confirmed bachelor until Rose finally said, yes."

"I know it will work out," said Gia. "Maybe next year."

"Yes. A lot can happen in a year," said Paul.

He turned to the tables with boxes of items marked by lot number.

"You bidding on anything?" he asked.

"The Royal Worcester. There aren't too many chipped plates and the glazing is good. We should be able to sell those for replacement plates without much trouble."

At home later that evening Gia poured each of them a cup of Earl Gray tea, and while David worked on paperwork he had brought home from the office, she opened Meg's notebook.

"Do you know anyone with the initials EDM?" she asked David when she noticed the initials repeated several times in the book.

"Are you sure they're someone's initials?" David asked and he lowered his papers. "What do you have there?"

Reluctant to tell David she had taken something from Meg's house, Gia didn't respond, but instead studied the page.

"It may not be initials of a person."

"Then it could be a term used in Parliament. EDM stands for Early Day Motion."

"What does that mean?" asked Gia.

"If you tell me what you're looking at, I may be able to give you a better explanation."

Gia considered telling him, but she knew he'd suggest she take it straight to Detective Inspector Barrett and she wasn't ready to do that.

"Notes. Notes on what's happening in Glasten," she said.

David looked at her without speaking for a moment as if deciding whether to tell her to stay out of whatever trouble was going on in the little hamlet.

His sigh was one of reluctant resignation. "It means it's up for debate in Parliament."

"Parliament can decide what happens to the village?"

"Not really. EDMs don't really have much outcome," said David. "But it will get attention and publicity for the village. They rarely actually get debated."

"What would be their argument?" asked Gia.

David had returned his gaze to the papers in front of him. He looked it up. "The argument would be, if the college went ahead with the sale and people bought houses as second homes it would be devastating to the community, which it would. Those houses would be empty most of the time, especially in the winter. It's a thriving community at the moment with its farms and there are several artisans."

Gia agreed. "I saw someone carving driftwood when I was there," said Gia. "So, there's hope?" she asked.

"There's always hope," responded David, but Gia wasn't sure they were still talking about Glasten.

Chapter 11

It had been a week since Meg was found and Gia was still no closer to finding out what had happened. She wondered if D.I. Barrett had uncovered anything. No one had reported seeing Collin. Holly was working at the hotel in Truro for a few hours as a trial run and Gia for the second time that week would go to the hotel, but first she needed to help Rose and Susan restock the shelves in the storage room. She slung her oversized bag over her shoulder and had reached the driveway when she spotted she had a flat tire.

"Darn," she kicked the tire and then took a good look at the green Volkswagen Golf.

She'd had it for years. Too many. It broke down occasionally and things fell off. She knew she should look for something new. But for now, she needed to get the tire fixed. Paul had already left and Rose wouldn't be much help.

She opened her phone and called David.

"Take my car," he said.

David, after he and Paul had worked on the MG sports car that David had bought more as a renovation hobby than to drive daily, began driving in it to work and his Lexus had been confined to the garage.

"I can't," said Gia. "You know how I am."

And they both did. Gia tended to run into things, once drove around on a flat tire for miles and bent the rim on one of the wheels and was simply clumsy.

"And it's got leather seats," she added.

"Might be protected a bit more, then," he said with a laugh. "The keys are hanging on the hook in the kitchen."

David trusted her with his car. Was he generous or what?

"I'm going to stop by and see Holly at the hotel. Can you get away for lunch?" she asked.

"I'd love to, but I've got a lot to get through today. Have fun."

Gia had unhooked the keys and was lovingly stroking the silver key fob with a large "L" engraved. A Lexus. Now if she could just reverse from the garage without hitting anything.

"Does David know you're driving his car?" asked Rose when she met Gia at the door of Lowenna Antiques.

"It will make a better family car," said Susan.

Gia still hadn't got used to Susan's red hair and she didn't respond immediately.

"More room for a car seat," added Rose.

"We're waiting," said Gia.

"What do you mean, Gia?" asked Susan. "Waiting for what?" She looked out the window as if expecting a stork to land on top of the Lexus.

"David and I have decided to wait for a year or two."

Rose was about to speak, but decided against it and instead shook her head from side to side and crunched her lips together so tightly they almost disappeared.

"We'll say no more about it, then," said Rose. She turned to Susan. "Are you going to help with all these boxes or not?"

Susan had been hovering from foot to foot and twisting her hands. Before following Rose into the storage room, she reached over and squeezed Gia's hand. A sign of encouragement each of them gave each other.

There, she'd said it. Now perhaps everyone would leave her alone. Things would get better now, but they didn't immediately because she looked out the window and watched, not a stork, but a flock of seagulls land on David's car.

"Oh no," said Susan following Gia's gaze. "I hope they don't leave little poopies."

Gia mentally added car wash to the list of things she needed to do and joined the two ladies in the tiny storage room.

Before driving into Truro, Gia decided to stop and see Beryl. She drove through Lowenna, taking a side road where she saw the village nestled in the center of a dip in rolling hills. Along the road was a Cornish wall with small rectangular blocks of Cornish slate stacked in a chevron design packed with soil and held together with flowers and weeds.

Beyond the wall was a thirteenth century Norman church with a square tower. Her car crunched over parched ground, past a tree with a gnarled bole and limbs sprouting haphazardly.

Bailey bounded to meet her and sat on his haunches while she scratched him behind the ear. He led the way to Beryl's house. She was clipping red roses that were held by a trellis around the front door to her cottage.

"Come on in," she said. "Tea's already brewing."

Gia followed Beryl into the kitchen.

"Look what I found," she said, handing Gia a handful of creased and tattered pages.

"What is it?" asked Gia.

"A petition. Meg was collecting names. I knew if I kept looking I'd find it. I also found her laptop, but I don't know anything about computers. Do you want to take it? There might be more about what she was doing on there."

Gia didn't immediately take the silver computer that Beryl was holding.

"We really should tell D.I. Barrett," said Gia.

Don't get involved. She heard David's voice in her head.

"It wouldn't hurt to take a look though would it?" asked Beryl.

She sat at the worn and scrubbed wooden table and opened the laptop while Beryl poured tea and brought in two mugs.

"It needs charging," Gia said.

"Take it with you," suggested Beryl.

It did look similar to Susan's and she may have a cord to charge the battery.

"I'll take a look, but after that I need to give it to the detective," Gia said, satisfied in her mind that she was doing the right thing.

"Where did you find it?" Gia asked and began looking at the list of names on the petition. "You didn't go back in Collin's cottage did you?"

Beryl nodded. "I didn't see any harm and I needed dog food for Bailey."

The dog wagged his tail at the sound of his name.

She decided to tell Beryl she'd met with Philip Hodges, the reporter.

After explaining what he had told her, Beryl leaned back on the scarred wooden chair.

"So, everything was fine until someone at the college tried to sell the estate? When was it transferred to the college as owners? Or can a trustee sell the estate?"

"I don't know how trusts work. A solicitor helped me when my aunt died and left me a house. I'll see if he can help. He may be able to shed some light on this."

"Oh, would you check with him?" asked Beryl. "I really am at my wit's end as to what to do and I think most people in the village have given up. Some of those with short tenancies have already moved out. I'm worried that this is going to end up like a ghost town. You know this place has been here for hundreds of years. It was listed in the Domesday Book and that was completed in the eleventh century."

"It makes you wonder what it will be like here in ten or twenty years. Look at Truro."

"I do like that there are more pedestrian areas," said Beryl, "But it's not a small town any more. Even after Queen Victoria gave Truro city status, it still remained a small hub for surrounding villages. Every time a new supermarket or store comes in, the buildings get bigger and bigger and all those houses down by the river. . ." She paused and they both nodded. "It used to be such a nice walk along there. There was nothing around except that little pub in Malpas with a few cottages. Meg wanted to preserve what she called our heritage. I'm not sure Martyn felt the same way."

"Have you seen anything of Meg's fiancé?" asked Gia.

"He hasn't been around for ages. It's a wonder she didn't ask him to buy the village if it was for sale. Ten million pounds would be a drop in the ocean to his family."

"Perhaps she had."

"She didn't really talk much. Don't get me wrong, we were good neighbors and we'd have a cup of tea occasionally, but she wasn't one to sit and talk about what was going on in her life and she never talked about Martyn."

Gia thought this odd as Beryl was a friendly sort and the hamlet cottages were so close together it would be difficult not to come into contact with each other during the day.

"I'm headed to Truro," said Gia, standing. "I'll take the laptop. Are you going to try and get more signatures on the petition?"

Beryl said she was and Gia left, avoiding ducks that waddled across her path.

It wasn't until she saw the spires of Truro cathedral that she realized she hadn't mentioned to Beryl the Early Day Motion up for debate in Parliament.

She hardly recognized Holly who stood behind the bar reading a book. She was wearing a white collared shirt and black pencil skirt. Her hair was tied back.

"How's it going?" asked Gia and slid onto a bar stool.

"I'm bored out of my mind," said Holly, laying the open book face down on the bar.

"Who died?" Gia nodded toward the black skirt.

"We have to wear black. I was told this was an upscale hotel. Obviously not to be confused with the downscale pub that I usually work at."

Holly poured orange juice into a glass and added club soda. She peeled a paper serviette from a stack she had in her hand and placed it on the bar before putting the glass down.

"Nice touch," said Gia.

"Guess, who's staying here?" asked Holly and stuffed the remaining serviettes under the bar.

"Who?" asked Gia, thinking it was pointless trying to guess.

"Martyn Baker."

"Meg's fiancé?"

"I think he did it? He's with a woman."

'Staying here with a woman?" Gia wanted to know.

"Yes. You would think he'd be in mourning. Not booking into a hotel with a . . ." she paused for effect. ". . . woman."

"Men don't like to be on their own," observed Gia. "Usually they find someone new quickly."

"I still think you should call D.I. Barrett and tell him," said Holly.

"And what do you think he would say to that?" asked Gia. "He wants physical evidence. The more I think about it, the more I think Meg's death had something to do with the sale of Glasten. While I'm in Truro I may as well go and see Mr. Alderton and see if he knows anything about the trust and if there's anything the villagers can do legally."

The gold plate of Barton & Alderton, Solicitors was placed neatly by the large oak door between a bakery and pub. Outside, smells of beer mingled with freshly baked bread, but inside there was the clean smell of freshly painted walls.

"He's expecting you," said the receptionist and she nodded toward an elegant staircase that wound its wide stairs around to the next floor.

Gia thanked her and at the top of the stairs, followed the slate blue carpet along dark hallways until she reached Mr. Alderton's office. Her eyes took a moment to adjust to the bright light from a large picture window after the darkness of the hallway.

"What can I do for you, Gia?" asked the solicitor and indicated the chair across from his desk.

"Have you heard that there is talk of selling the Glasten Estate?"

"I've been following that story," he said.

"Meg Penhallow had been the leader of the village in trying to get it to remain as it is."

"That was the young woman who was killed?"

"Yes."

"And what's your interest, Gia?" Mr. Alderton leaned forward and steepled his fingers.

What was her interest? She wanted to protect the home of Bailey, a dog. That didn't sound compelling. But the truth was, she hated to see change, hated to see a whole village disappear. She'd fought the owners of a crematorium last year who wanted to encroach on gardens that were now a popular spot for visitors and locals alike.

"Gia?" Mr. Alderton asked when there was no response.

"I don't like change?"

"None of us do," he said.

"I know it sounds silly, because I'm not from here. I wasn't born here. But I'm part of the community now. The tenants have lived there for generations and it's simply not fair that they have to find somewhere else to live. The children will have to go to other schools. The villagers whose families have been brought up together will be split up and what will happen to the land?"

"I believe there's over three thousand acres as part of the estate." He peered at her. "You're always looking for a cause," he stated.

Was she?

"Going to battle for friends," he added.

She supposed he was right. Anything that crossed her path, she seemed to latch on to and hang on until the battle was over.

"It's what Mr. Gillard wanted too. His wishes were clear in his will. He wanted it to stay the same with the tenants taken care of," said Gia.

"You've seen his will?" asked the solicitor.

"No. It's what I've heard. I thought perhaps you could access a copy of the will. That's really what I wanted to ask you."

"It's the trust we need to be concerned with," said Mr. Alderton. "As I said, I've been following what's going on. Mr. Gillard trusted the college to take care of his wishes to preserve the estate, but he chose the wrong trustee and with the way the trust is written with no end date or a beneficiary, I'm doubtful it's even valid."

"What does that mean? They have to sell it someone else?"

"Why don't you leave it with me? It's an interesting case. Stop by in a few days and we'll see if we can do anything to help the tenants."

"Bless you," said Gia.

And she meant it. He'd helped her to keep Aunt Grace's cottage. He'd helped her when she had nowhere to turn.

In her pocket her phone beeped.

"Go ahead and take it," said Mr. Alderton. "I have a client waiting. We'll talk in a few days."

Gia hit the button and Mr. Alderton began making notes on his pad.

"Can you come and get me?" said Holly breathlessly.

"What's wrong with your car?"

"Maximo brought me. Can you come? Now?"

"Where are you?" asked Gia.

"Outside the hotel."

Gia looked at her watch. Holly still had more than an hour to work before lunch time closing.

"Can you?"

"I'll be right there, but —"

Holly had already disconnected and Gia rushed out to her car.

When she arrived, Holly was standing in a shop doorway next to the hotel. Her hair was disheveled and her white shirt had a large wet brown stain. She ran to the car and climbed in, slamming the door.

"What on earth happened to you?" asked Gia.

"Just go. I'll tell you on the way home," said Holly. "Go. Go." Holly slammed her open palm on the dashboard for emphasis.

When they had driven up the hill and Gia could see the church spires in her rear view mirror growing smaller and smaller, she glanced sideways at her friend.

"Are you going to tell me what happened?"

"Why are you driving David's car?" Holly pulled the band from her hair and fluffed it out with her fingertips.

"I have a flat tire. But never mind that. What happened?"

"Martyn Barker."

"He did that to you?" Gia wanted to know.

"Not exactly."

"Holly, if you don't tell me what happened, I'm pulling over right now."

Gia looked for a place to stop, but the lanes were too narrow and there was nowhere to pull in.

Holly tugged at her wet shirt. "He came in with that tart and I lost it."

This wasn't good. Once Holly was angry enough to reach the point of no return, it was never a pretty sight.

"How did you get wet?"

"I dunked water all over him and the tart he was with threw her beer at me. Then she grabbed my hair."

"What started it?"

Holly looked out the window and Gia could see her biting the inside of her cheek. Her shirt was so wet, it was dripping.

"Holly?"

"I accused him of killing Meg."

"Oh no. Why?"

"I had a feeling he did it."

"What did he say?"

"I didn't believe him," said Holly.

"Didn't believe what? You're not making any sense."

"He said they'd broken up two weeks ago and he'd been in London until the week-end."

"Aren't you supposed to be working?" asked Gia.

"I'm not going back. It was a mutual agreement."

Gia doubted it was mutual.

"I was so bored there."

"Sounds like you livened things up. Do you think he really was away?"

"I hate to say it, but I think I may have been mistaken."

"Did you apologize?"

Holly looked at her with a startled look. "Have you lost your mind?"

That was a silly question. Of course Holly hadn't apologized. Even though she had said she was wrong, she would never admit it to Martyn Baker.

"Who was the woman?" asked Gia.

"He said it was his secretary."

"A standard response."

"So, who do you think killed her, then?" asked Holly rapidly brushing the tangles from her hair.

"I don't know," said Gia and slowed down. Holly's outburst had an effect on her foot on the pedal and she'd taken a turn too quickly. She patted the dashboard as if assuring the Lexus she would drive carefully from now on.

"He also said they'd picked up Collin," said Holly.

"I don't think it was him either, but where was he?"

"He'd gone to Hampshire to talk to the director at the college."

"We need to go and see him and see what he found out," said Gia. "I just talked to Mr. Alderton, he's going to look into the trust and see if there's anything to be done legally."

She emphasized the word *legally*.

"I may have gone a bit overboard," admitted Holly.

"You think? I also talked to Beryl. She's trying to get more signatures on the petition she found in Meg's room. And . . ."

Holly stopped brushing and turned to Gia.

"I sense I wasn't the one doing something *illegal*," Holly emphasized the word just as Gia had done.

". . . I have Meg's computer."

"D.I. Barrett isn't going to be pleased."

She was sure of that. He tended to get upset when she interfered with his investigations.

"We need to take a look at that computer," said Holly.

"We do, but first I need to get David's car washed."

But they did neither because Rose called and said she needed help in the shop.

"She's gone off on that boat again," said Rose when Gia reached Lowenna Antiques. "I've been busy all afternoon."

Gia looked over at an empty space where candles had once been stacked.

"Holidaymakers like to take those home as presents. That was a good idea of yours to put a map of Cornwall on the label."

"So, Susan went fishing again?" asked Gia.

"They're out chasing tuna. I don't think they'll find any more do you? The one Susan caught must have been lost."

They didn't have the opportunity to talk further as the shop bell tinkled constantly during the remainder of the afternoon. Last minute souvenirs for friends and relatives were bought. Gia found another box of candles and put those on display. The rack that had key rings, bottle openers with shapes of anchors, mine air shafts, and pictures of Lowenna looked like a Christmas tree depleted of decorations.

It was six o'clock when the customers began to dwindle and Rose placed a tray with tea pot and cups on the table. At a few minutes after six, the door burst opened and there stood Susan. Her red hair sprouted from the bun on her head like loose springs. Her face had a color that Gia thought was a tinge of green and she held a handkerchief to her mouth.

"I'm never getting on a boat again," she said and slumped into the chair that Gia pulled out for her.

Rose shook her head slowly as if she didn't have the energy to voice her thoughts.

"Did they find any tuna?" asked Gia.

"No. But John and Percy are going out again tomorrow."

"Do you want me to take you home?" asked Gia.

"I don't want to be any trouble," said Susan and dropped her head on to the table with such force that the tea cups rattled.

Rose still shook her head from side to side, but no sound came from her lips.

Gia and Susan left Rose to lock up the shop and the two of them walked across the road to the car park.

"You didn't get the poopies off David's car," said Susan. "Won't he be upset?" she asked.

"David never gets upset," said Gia and meant it.

"Nice leather seats," said Susan feeling the tan leather with her small hand as if it were a pet cat.

Gia pulled from the car park and crossed the bridge.

"You should get it cleaned before he sees it though. What's that smell?" said Susan and touched a wet spot left by Holly's dripping shirt. She brought her hand to her nose. "It smells like beer."

And it was at that point, Gia turned a corner and she heard Susan make a small sound before vomiting all over David's nice leather seats.

"Where's my car," said David when Gia walked up the driveway.

He was bent down, changing the tire on her Volkswagen.

"As a special treat. I'm getting it detailed for you," she said. "I'll pick it up in the morning."

"What did you do?" he asked not unkindly.

"I didn't do anything. I'm just getting it cleaned for you."

That was an honest answer. She hadn't actually done anything. It was the birds. It was Susan. It was Holly. But *she* hadn't caused any of the problems for once.

Chapter 12

Gia awoke and stared at the neon numbers on the bedside clock without deciphering shapes. Sun shone through the slatted blinds leaving a shadow of lines on the wall. At first she was disoriented. Lighter than usual when she woke up, she looked back at the clock. It was nine and she needed to help Rose in the shop this morning. The front door closed. David had already left.

There was coffee and a note by the bed. *Hope you wake up before this gets cold – Love you.*

Another week and this would be over. David hopefully will do well in the triathlon and then they could get back to normal life whatever that was.

While she sipped her morning drink, Gia grabbed index cards that she'd been using as bookmarks.

Canute and Daisy lay in the bedroom. Canute had one paw across Daisy's chest and Canute let out soft snores. Daisy sounded like a door opening and closing with an occasional squeak. Neither moved when she walked past them. The coffee was still warm and she took it with her while she popped two slices of bread in the toaster and shrugged into a cardigan over her long t-shirt. There was a chill in the air and a mist hung like a veil along the coast. She took a moment to sit and enjoy her toast slathered with marmalade before dressing.

Staring at the blank cards, Gia thought about the past week and whom she had come in contact with after Meg's death.

She wrote *Collin Penhallow* on the first card and listed motives for killing his sister. Perhaps he hadn't shared her enthusiasm for saving the farm. From what she had heard, he also didn't like to think of his sister marrying. Had that sparked an argument which resulted in Meg falling? It could have been an accident after all. But if she had simply fallen and cut her head, then why hadn't he called for an ambulance and why would he leave her in the car park? Even if it had been Collin, how would he have moved his sister from the cottage?

Gia continued listing motives and questions on the card. Next she thought of Martyn Barker. Had he been upset about the breakup? Could that have sparked an argument? Perhaps his family hadn't known Meg and Martyn were separated and wanted to make sure the marriage plans didn't continue.

She put the card headed *Martyn Barker* aside and turned next to a blank card where she noted *Retirement Community*. Who were the people behind that? Would they be desperate enough to stop Meg's efforts to save the farms and the estate?

And there was another suspect. The college itself. If the institution was able to sell the estate, it stood to make millions, rather than the paltry rents currently received by the college.

Gia swigged back the rest of her coffee, pulled on her jeans and t-shirt and while still pondering suspects in Meg's death, she left the cottage.

Her Volkswagen Golf looked sadder each day and she chose to walk down the cliff road. Besides, she still had to pick up David's car which she planned to do later that morning.

When she reached the bottom of the hill, across from the church, she saw Collin standing by the rose arbor. He straddled his motor bike and zoomed off through Lowenna.

Didn't Holly say the police had picked him up? She'd call D.I. Barrett and ask what was going on. But then she had another thought. He probably wouldn't tell her anything. She'd call Beryl instead, which she did later that morning while Rose and Susan fussed over morning coffee. Beryl picked the phone up after the first ring.

"I saw Collin in Lowenna this morning," said Gia after they'd exchanged pleasantries.

"He's back at the cottage. The police had him in for questioning and then let him go," said Beryl.

"But there's nothing in the cottage. He can't live there."

There was no response and then she heard Beryl clear her throat. "Actually, he's staying with me."

Gia could read all kinds of things into this statement, but the truth was Collin and Beryl had been neighbors, they'd grown up together and the small hamlet was like a family.

"He went to visit Martyn's parents after he went to the college," said Beryl. "He thought they might be able to stop the sale of the village. They're very influential. It was Martyn's suggestion."

Holly was going to be upset when she found out she had made a fool of herself. Martyn wouldn't be helping Collin if he had been the one who killed Meg would he? Or he could be doing it because of guilt. So she didn't feel she could entirely cross him off her suspect list.

Susan placed a tray on the table with coffee cups and biscuits and Gia finished her call, promising to let Beryl know if she heard anything.

"Percy and John are going out again this morning," said Susan. "If there was one tuna there has to be more, don't you think?"

Her question was to Gia, who Susan would be disappointed to know, didn't have all the answers.

It was Rose who responded. "It looks like another storm is coming in. I hope they get back before it comes crashing down."

"They know what they're doing, Rose," said Susan with more bravado than she usually showed. "John and Percy are both good fishermen."

"They must be back," said Gia. "Look. There's John's boat in the harbor."

"It was the Mermaid, they went on," said Susan.

Which left Gia wondering if a charter boat was the best craft to be in when caught in a storm.

Later that morning when Gia left to pick up David's car, the mist had cleared, but Rose had been right, the clouds were dark gray and looked angry as if at any moment they would start banging against each other and Thor, the god of thunder, would appear between them. It was probably not the best day to get a car detailed, but for now it looked pristine and smelled wonderful. She drove back to the car park and wondered if she should stick a scare crow out there to keep the seagulls away.

"Looks a treat," said Susan when Gia returned. "David will be pleased. Sorry about the accident I had yesterday."

Gia was thankful David hadn't seen the car that usually spent its days in the garage. He would not have thought it *looked a treat* when it was covered with seagull droppings and what Susan liked to refer to as her *accident*. She was quite getting used to Susan's red hair and she noticed this morning she was wearing lilac colored eye shadow and a little mascara.

"God loves fishermen," said Susan. "Fish were the first creatures created."

"She's got it bad, this time," whispered Rose. "I hope he doesn't drop down dead or something."

"Is David going to keep going with this running business, Gia?" asked Susan while she busied herself with waving her feather duster around and causing Gia to sneeze.

It was Rose who answered. "He doesn't have time for all that nonsense. He must be getting something out of his system. One more week. Right, Gia?"

Gia nodded. "One more week. Next Saturday is the race. If there are as many people as last year, I expect we will have over two hundred people running."

"There's Iris," said Susan and tapped on the window.

"Doesn't look good out there," said Iris when she burst into the shop. "The wind is up to fifty five miles per hour in places and a twister was spotted off Tintagel."

Gia had never seen Iris look as anxious as she did now.

"We don't have tornadoes in England," stated Rose.

"We do. They usually don't touch ground," said Susan. "But there were thirty or forty last year. I read it on the internet."

Susan didn't show her usual enthusiasm when quoting from the internet and her face showed worry lines to mirror Iris's.

"Didn't John check the forecast before he left this morning?" asked Gia.

"He did, but he said it was sure to be nothing. They are both on this quest to find those stupid tuna."

Gia didn't think the tuna were stupid as they were avoiding being caught. That is, if there were any off the coast of Cornwall.

"Have a cup of coffee," said Rose. "Take a pew."

Iris sat and hovered her hand over the biscuit tin, then changed her mind.

"My tummy is a bit upset this morning," said Iris.

"We've got peppermint tea," offered Gia who had bought some when she hadn't felt well.

"That would be lovely," said Iris.

"Hope you don't have the virus that Gia and I had. It can be a bit tough on the tummy," said Susan.

"Can't you reach them by radio?" asked Rose.

"I tried, but they're not answering," said Iris.

Susan stood by the door watching the clouds anxiously.

"But," said Susan. "They'll be all right won't they? John's been in storms before hasn't he?"

"Nothing like what's brewing out there now," said Iris.

"Better put on some more lights, Susan," said Rose. "It's getting dark in here."

As if connected to the sky, when Susan hit the light switch a burst of thunder trembled.

Gia could see tears well in Susan's eyes. She walked over to her and draped her arm around her little friend's slender shoulders. The lights flickered and when they finally came back on Gia steered Susan toward the table.

"Come and have a cup of coffee," said Gia. "I didn't tell you what happened to Holly yesterday," she said with an attempt at levity.

"What was that girl thinking?" said Rose after Gia told them of Holly's encounter with Martyn Barker. "His family has money. She could end up with a law suit. GBH."

"Grievous bodily harm," said Susan. "I've been watching Law and Order U.K. I love that Detective Ronnie Brooks." Her chin dipped toward her chest. "Not a patch on my Percy, though."

"What about music?" suggested Gia, but the music was interrupted by an announcement about the storm.

"Is David at home?" asked Rose. "He's not still out running is he?"

They had all been thinking of the fishermen and Gia hadn't thought about David, but surely he would be home by now. She picked up the phone.

It was then that the music stopped, the lights went out again and Susan screamed.

"He's going to die," shouted Susan and they all shivered.

"That was quite a storm," said Holly when Gia stopped by the King William for lunch.

"David told me he got soaked," said Gia.

"I hope he doesn't get sick. After all the training he's done it would be awful if he couldn't compete. At least most of the boats are in the harbor. I don't think anyone went out this morning. People were in here complaining that their charters were cancelled."

"John and Percy went out," said Gia.

"On their own?" asked Holly.

"I think so."

"Hopefully, they pulled into a cove to ride out the storm or surely they found another harbor along the coast," Holly leaned on her elbows.

"Let's hope so. Susan was beside herself. Are you going out with Max tonight?" asked Gia.

"Probably."

"You don't sound very excited?"

"He's nice enough, but he's a bit boring. He's all about business and always asking me questions."

"What business? You've never said what he does."

"Retirement villages," said Holly. "His company, and I say *his* company because his family owns it, wants to put in a golf course and community village."

"Let me guess, he's looking at Glasten too?" asked Gia.

"Looks like it."

"Gosh, everyone's after that little hamlet."

"Have you looked at the laptop yet?" asked Holly and scooped up empty glasses and placed them under the counter.

"No, but I've got in the car. The battery needs charging."

"Go and get it. It's slowing down a bit in here. I'll look in the office and see if Barry has his computer here. We may be able to use his cord to plug it in. We can take a look."

Gia left Holly giving directions to a patron, but Holly was waving her hands in all directions and the couple looked puzzled.

When she opened up the laptop and plugged it in, Gia was surprised that there was no password required and she was able to look at the history of internet searches.

"See if you can look at her e-mails," suggested Holly.

Gia paused and rubbed her tummy.

"You still not feeling good?"

"It's not that I'm feeling badly. I just feel odd," said Gia.

"Well you've always been odd," said Holly. "Did you find anything?"

"Meg had saved her login information and password. Here are some e-mails from Martyn."

Gia swiveled the computer on the bar so that both of them could look. She opened the last e-mail from Martyn.

"Well, I guess he was telling the truth," said Holly. "They had broken up. But he seems very friendly in that e-mail for someone who'd been jilted."

"There doesn't seem anything here," said Gia.

She returned to the history of internet searches and clicked on the first few.

"That's interesting," she said. "Look at this. Henry Rogerson, the college director, was trying to sell the land to a sewage plant not a wind turbine company. No wonder Meg was so upset. That's got to be worse to lose your home to sewage."

"I think I saw Rogerson on some of those e-mails. Go back and look," said Holly. "Sort them by name and we can see all the communications from him."

But when Gia returned to the e-mail screen, it wasn't his name that caught her eye, but another familiar name on Meg's e-mail list and she wondered why the two of them were having any contact with each other.

"You better get over here," said Rose frantically when Gia answered her mobile phone. "I don't know what to do with Susan."

In the background Gia could hear what sounded like an injured cat.

"What *is* that noise," Gia asked.

"Susan." said Rose. "They've got the coastguard out looking for John and Percy. There's been no contact from them."

Iris burst into the shop, clutching her mobile phone as if it were a lifeline.

"There's been reports of gale force nine winds," said Iris.

"Have you heard anything about John and Percy?" asked Rose.

Susan was mumbling, but no one could understand her. She paced back and forth the length of the small shop.

Iris slumped into a chair.

"From what I understand, the Mermaid was taking on water. The lifeboat crew were out on another call and found them. They were able to get a salvage pump on board and are towing it into harbor."

"Here?" asked Rose peering out the window at the harbor wall.

"No. Farther down the coast. But . . ." Iris paused and glanced at Susan who was nearing the back of the shop and lowered her voice. "Percy was washed overboard. He may have been picked up by another vessel. The boat couldn't get close to the Mermaid and they must have called the coast guard, but there's hope that they saw Percy and picked him up."

"Is John still on the boat?" asked Rose.

"No. A rescue helicopter from the Royal Naval Air Station, Culdrose was able to lift him from the boat. We'll know more when they get back. I'm waiting to find out what hospital they're taking him to." Iris checked her phone for missed calls.

"Susan," said Rose. "Do sit down, you're making me dizzy. They've got the coast guard, the navy and the lifeboat out there. We'll be hearing something soon."

But Rose looked at Gia and shook her head and both of them wondered if what they heard would be good news.

Chapter 13

"What are you doing?" asked David when he sat at the table and they both watched the television in the corner of the room, hoping for news of Percy. "Thanks for making breakfast, Gia."

David spread butter over the burnt toast, leaving behind small black specks on the butter.

Gia absently sipped coffee and spread index cards on the table and didn't answer.

David picked one up.

"Isn't this Holly's new boyfriend?" David asked knowing that there was always a necessity to distinguish between current boyfriends and previous ones.

He turned the card over. "Gia?"

"I'm just trying to help D.I. Barrett. He's at a crossroads in the investigation."

"And the Devon and Cornwall police force can't manage without you?"

"Everyone could do with a little help," said Gia. "Aren't you running today?"

"No. You have me all to yourself, but you look like you're busy."

Gia shuffled the cards together and placed them in a stack on the table.

"I can do this later. What do you want to do?"

"How about we go for a drive?" he suggested. "Perhaps to Porthcurno."

"Wonderful," said Gia.

A whole day with David, a Sunday drive, and a walk among the coastal gardens. Perfect.

While she popped the cards into her bag, David tossed his toast into the rubbish bin.

Travelling south west toward Penzance, David drove with one hand on the wheel and the other holding Gia's. They followed the road along the coast and Gia spotted St. Michael's Mount with its priory perched on top. The island was joined to the mainland by a causeway that disappeared at high tide and it was on the beach across from the island a few years ago that Gia first realized she was falling in love with David. She sighed with contentment.

"Did mum decide to close the shop today?" asked David when he pulled in to the Minack Theatre entrance.

"She stayed with Susan last night. There was no point being in the shop with Susan in such a state."

"Still no sign of Percy, then?" asked David.

But they had both watched the news and there had been no phone calls. David knew he hadn't been found.

"I haven't heard any more," said Gia.

"Let's hope for the best."

Yes, they would hope for the best but fear the worst, because if the ship that was close to the Mermaid had picked up Percy and contacted the coast guard, surely they would have mentioned it.

"We really should come here and see a play," said David when they walked down the stone steps and sat overlooking the stage and beyond that the sea.

"It reminds me of a Roman amphitheatre," said Gia. "But did you know that the woman who built this theatre on the side of the cliffs was from Derbyshire."

They watched seagulls swoop and dive over the cliffs. Gia thought about their, or rather her, decision to wait a year or two before committing to bringing a child into their home. But on a day like this with David to herself, she wondered if she would ever be ready for children and if she did want to share her husband with someone else. She looped her arm through his and leaned her head on his shoulder. Wind blew her hair and she closed her eyes, but could still see the bright sunshine through her eyelids.

"Rowena Cade bought this land for a hundred pounds and built a house that she shared with her mother," continued Gia. "They put on plays in the summer and then she had an idea to build a theatre here overlooking the sea. Quite an amazing woman."

"Rowena's a nice name, don't you think?"

David spoke quietly and Gia wondered if he was just thinking out loud. A nice name in general or was he considering children's names – their child's name? She let go of his arm and brushed her hair from her face.

"Do you want to walk through the gardens?" she asked and without waiting for a response began edging her way toward the stone steps.

"That was lovely," said Gia when they walked back to the car. "How do they get all those plants to grow so profusely close to the sea?"

"Didn't you see the sign?" asked David. "They were all salt tolerant plants. Next year I want to work on the garden."

"We can work on it together," said Gia who hadn't had much interest in the garden since Aunt Grace's death.

Gia closed her eyes for a moment lulled by the sound of the engine and the smooth road. They were not far from Lowenna when she opened them.

"Thanks, David," she said.

"For what?"

"A lovely day."

In response, he brushed his hand softly against her cheek and smiled.

Pulling out her hair brush, Gia noticed the index cards in her bag.

"Do you want to help me with this?" she asked holding up the cards.

"Gia."

"Please. You're good at figuring things out."

"Okay, then."

"This is what I've got so far." Gia turned over the first index card. "Facts. Meg was injured or killed at the farmhouse. Her blood was on the cushion of the settee that Collin threw out."

"Do you know that?"

"D.I. Barrett said it was her blood. She was driven by car to the car park," Gia continued.

"You don't know that," said David.

"Well, Collin could hardly have put her on the back of his motor bike and if someone dragged her, there would be evidence of that on her body."

"Did John Barrett tell you that too?"

"No. I looked at her body, remember? Her clothes would have been torn if she'd been dragged."

"Good point."

"Holly's boyfriend, Max, is here on behalf of his family who want to buy Glasten."

"What will they do with it?"

"The retirement community that mum and dad want to move to. So he has a motive, but he was with Holly on Thursday night, but she said she left him about eleven o'clock so if it happened in the early hours it could have been him."

"What would he have been doing in Collin's house?" asked David.

"It was Meg's house too and the settee was in her room upstairs. He may have been going out with Meg as well as Holly."

"So, you're thinking he left Holly at eleven and went to see Meg."

"He's French," said Gia as if that answered the question. "Besides, he wanted Meg to stop trying to save the village."

136

"You're forgetting one thing," said David. "Meg was engaged to Martyn Barker."

"They broke up."

"And you know this how?" asked David.

Wondering whether to confess to taking Meg's laptop Gia didn't answer straight way, but by then she didn't have to because they heard the drone of a coast guard helicopter and stopped to look.

"Looks like a boat on the rocks," said Gia peering over the cliff. "Lucky it wasn't the Mermaid."

"It must have happened during the storm," suggested David. "Look they're bringing someone up on a winch. Are you all right?"

Gia's face had turned pale and she stared at the stretcher as they lowered it.

"It's Percy," she said. "And he's not moving."

Chapter 14

None of the ladies from Lowenna Antiques attended the knitting circle meeting on Monday morning. Gia worked alone at the shop. Susan was distraught and Rose had stayed with her all night. The two of them walked in the door just as Gia had finished serving a customer. She was shocked at Susan's appearance. If it was possible, Susan seemed to have shrunk into a wizened old lady overnight. Her red hair was disheveled and her bun had fallen over her right ear.

"Come and sit down," said Gia, pulling out a chair.

"I'll just put the kettle on," said Rose, who as far as Gia could remember, had never boiled water at Lowenna Antiques before. She had in the past yelled for Susan to do it.

"I can . . ." Susan started to rise, but Rose put her hand firmly on her friend's shoulder.

"You just sit there. You're in no fit state to brew tea."

Gia hovered, not knowing what to do, but feeling that just sitting there and thinking about poor Percy was about the worst suggestion anyone could have.

"Do you want to start listing the plates that Collin brought in?" Gia asked Susan.

Rose grabbed her arm. "What *is* wrong with you?" she whispered. "She doesn't need to be doing anything. Look at her." Rose nodded toward Susan whose head was bobbing slowly and she began rocking to and fro in her chair.

"She needs to be kept busy to take her mind off what happened," Gia said louder than she had intended.

Susan didn't seem to notice.

Ignoring Rose, Gia dragged a box of plates toward the chair where Susan sat. She placed a pad of paper and pencil in front of her and began removing the newspaper wrapping.

"These are all Royal Copenhagen Christmas plates," said Gia. "Aunt Grace had some like these."

"Christmas," echoed Susan.

It wasn't a season Susan would be looking forward to now.

Rose banged a cup of coffee down so hard that the milky liquid slopped into the saucer. But Gia noticed that Susan's back had straightened, Her chin was no longer dipping down and she was studying each plate.

"It would be lovely to display some of these for Christmas," said Susan.

"You do know it's July don't you?" asked Rose.

"It will come quickly," said Susan.

"Well, let's not talk about Christmas now," said Rose. "Anyway, Collin is going to need some money for these as soon as possible. If he has to move, I doubt he has anything saved up judging by the state of the furniture that he threw out. What's David's plan for Saturday?" Rose asked Gia.

"They'll start off with swimming," said Gia.

As she pointed out the window where the race route had been planned, she noticed Ruth Rundle struggling along the street, moving her walker slowly in front of her. Again, when she got to the car, she straightened her back and tossed the walker in, then agilely climbed behind the steering wheel. Her suspicions had been confirmed. There was nothing wrong with that woman.

Gia continued unwrapping the Christmas plates for Susan to list. Each was bundled in newspaper and she noticed Philip Hodges' byline on an article. But it wasn't the article that held Gia's attention, it was a letter to him that was obviously a draft with notes and words crossed out and folded between the newspaper pages. The letter was from Meg and mentioned someone Gia had only briefly considered up until now as a murder suspect.

What Gia did know was that it was time to hand over the laptop and Meg's notebook to D.I. Barrett. She thought about confronting Collin but then decided against it. She would take it straight to the police station.

During a lull in customers that morning at Lowenna Antiques, Gia walked over to the King William and was surprised to see Holly leaning over the bar head to head with a man and it wasn't Max.

"Here we go again," whispered Gia under her breath, wishing her friend would find someone and settle down.

But when the man turned, Gia's face brightened and she almost skipped toward him.

"Brian! Where did you spring from?"

"Australia wasn't for me," said her cousin.

Gia looked around the room.

"He's on his own," said Holly brightly. "It didn't work out." She sounded almost relieved.

"Holly was telling me about the manor," said Brian.

"Things are getting clearer," said Gia.

"You found something?" asked Holly.

"I'm not sure. I want to look into a few things before I tell anyone," said Gia.

"Even me?" asked Holly.

"Especially you."

They both laughed, knowing Holly couldn't keep a secret.

"You haven't been getting into trouble again?" asked Brian.

"Just following up on a few leads," said Gia.

"You do know that you aren't part of the police force, don't you?" Brian couldn't decide whether to nod or shake his head and ended up doing both.

"So tell us about Australia," said Holly and leaned her elbow on the bar, supporting her head with the palm of her hand.

"Nice beaches," said Brian.

"We have nice beaches," said Gia.

"Sharks." said Brian.

"We have sharks," said Gia.

"Big sharks," said Brian.

Holly was watching the two of them spar backwards and forwards.

"We have tuna," said Gia.

"What?" asked Brian.

Holly jumped into the volley. "Susan caught a tuna."

Both Gia and Holly lowered their eyes, remembering the disastrous outcome of chasing tuna. Brian didn't notice and let out a loud belly laugh then turned to the two, taking in their solemn faces.

"Did something happen."

Holly explained that John and Percy had gone out to look for more tuna to see if they could get a commercial fishing license, but they hit a storm and Percy was killed.

"Can we find a Cornish dating service for you?" asked Gia, trying to think of a good way to segue between someone dying and Brian's latest effort to look for a girlfriend and finding none. "Perhaps keep you on home ground."

"No need," said Brian. "I'm not dating for at least a year. I'll just hang around friends for now. Holly's going to dinner with me tonight to make sure I don't go astray."

"Good for her," said Gia, but she looked at the two of them with suspicion. Was there more than friendship going on between them?

At least Brian was back. That was one less thing she had to worry about.

"Do you want to come with us to dinner?" asked Brian.

"I'm making dinner for David tonight," said Gia. "Rose has been teaching me how to cook."

Rose had given Gia a slow cooker and she marveled that she could stack beef, carrots, onions and potatoes in a pot in the morning, plug it in and dinner was ready when they arrived home.

"And anyway," said Holly. "Gia wouldn't stay awake for dinner. She falls asleep at the drop of a hat. Perhaps you have narcolepsy.

For once, there was no smoke in the kitchen, which usually happened when Gia cooked. Rose always joked that she knew when dinner was ready because she could hear the smoke alarm.

The table was set and Gia had put candles on the table.

David hugged her to him when he walked in the door.

"Smells delicious," he said, but without enthusiasm.

"It's not burnt," said Gia. "Look."

"I have a surprise for you," David said when she reached the kitchen. He waved an envelope in front of her, then snatched it away when she tried to grab it. "After dinner."

While they ate, they talked about their day. Gia avoided mentioning Susan and her loss. She couldn't imagine being without David and didn't want to think about it.

After they had eaten, Gia reached for the envelope that was propped on the table beside the wine bottle.

"Can I open it, now?"

David nodded. "When we went to the Minack Theatre the other day I thought that we needed to get away more often."

"Tintagel!" said Gia.

"After the race. I've booked us for two nights."

"Sunday and Monday?"

"I already checked with mum. She said she can manage the shop with Susan."

"And I can have you all to myself? No bicycle or running shoes involved."

"Yes. Just strolls across the cliffs and we can walk down to the castle."

David, Gia knew, was talking about where legend purported King Arthur's castle had once stood.

She hugged the reservation to her. Two days, two nights with David. No interruptions, no rushing off in the morning.

"Whose computer is that?" asked David.

Gia didn't answer immediately.

"Meg's," she finally said.

"Why do you have it?"

"I found it," said Gia.

"You found it by the side of the road?" said David sarcastically.

"Beryl went with me to Meg's cottage."

"Oh, Gia. That's evidence."

"I know and I'm taking to D.I. Barrett first thing in the morning. Promise."

And she intended to and as soon as she dropped it off at the police station, she would talk to Philip Hodges.

Chapter 15

The funeral party that misty morning, was sparse.

Inside the modern building, was an open beamed ceiling and a Cornish stone wall interrupted only by a wooden cross. The rest of the room was brilliant white reflecting light from overhead white fixtures hanging from the dark wood beams. It didn't seem a fitting place to memorialize the life of a fisherman.

Rose, Susan and Gia sat together in a row of blue cushioned chairs. All three of them stared at the closed coffin. Percy had no relatives, no family left except for his son who sat by Susan with an empty seat between them. The vicar talked about Percy and they found out things none of them had known. He liked to garden, liked to listen to classical music, liked to dance. None of these things he would be doing with Susan.

Susan, dressed head to toe in black, sobbed silently. Her shoulders shuddered.

And then it was over. They walked from the chapel with Susan flanked by her two friends. Percy's son declined to join them.

"Where will Percy go?" asked Susan.

"His ashes are to be scattered in the Garden of Remembrance," said Rose. "His son said his will was specific about that."

Susan nodded. "For the best," she said.

"Shall we stop at the Seahorse Café and get it cuppa?" asked Rose.

"Why don't we go to the pub?" suggested Gia. "I think what Susan needs is a brandy."

Susan didn't respond. She looked to her left and then her right as if undecided which way she should go.

At the King William, they sat Susan in the corner and Holly brought her a snifter of brandy. The other two ladies opted for shandy.

"Will she be all right?" Holly asked Gia.

"Susan may seem fragile, but she's resilient, and she'll bounce back," said Gia.

But as she said it, she wasn't so sure. She'd never seen Susan so sad, so deflated like the air had been let out of her.

"We'll just keep her busy," said Gia.

"That's best," said Holly. "By the way Beryl was in here with her petition. I'm worried that something might happen to her."

"Why," asked Gia.

"If whoever killed Meg gets wind of it, they might knock Beryl off too."

"I don't think it was anything to do with the estate," said Gia.

"You don't?" asked Holly. "But I thought you said they were connected?"

"I did, but I was wrong. I'll tell you by the end of the week."

"You're being very secretive. Do you know who did it?"

"Let me put it this way. I should know in a few days."

Gia rubbed her tummy.

"Are you still not feeling well?" asked Holly.

"It comes and goes."

"Promise me you'll go and see a doctor."

"Next week. Promise. After the triathlon. David has us booked into a hotel Sunday and Monday. I have an appointment with the doctor on Tuesday."

On Thursday morning, Gia drove to Truro and kept her appointment with Mr. Alderton.

"Were you able to find out anything that might help," she asked.

"Here's where we stand. Some of it you may already know. The Charity Commission has declared that the college can't own the property because it conflicts with their charity status and the Commission are requiring the college to sell the estate. I looked at the trust. Because the trust doesn't have an end date or a specific beneficiary, in that it runs indefinitely, it's invalid. So, for all intents and purposes the college can't sell the property because it doesn't own it."

"So, what are the tenants supposed to do?"

"What we might be able to do, if they want me to act on their behalf that is, ask the court to void the trust and revert to the original will in which Mr. Gillard wishes his wife and the tenants to be protected and allowed to live in the estate. Perhaps an option is to revert the property to Mrs. Gillard, then she herself can set up a trust. That's my suggestion."

And in Gia's opinion it sounded like a brilliant one. A college in Hampshire didn't have the best interests in either Mrs. Gillard or the tenant farms.

"I'll see if I can set up a meeting with everyone and let them know," said Gia. "The organization that was trying to make Glasten into a retirement community is going to be disappointed," said Gia.

"Not Sandy Dunes."

"Yes, my parents were looking into it. They, I mean my mother, was interested in having a golf course on her doorstep and my dad liked the idea of not having to mow the grass."

Mr. Alderton leaned forward. "That's a scam," he said.

"What do you mean."

"The troubles at Glasten have been well publicized and there are several organizations trying to benefit from the possible sale of the estate. Sandy Dunes has been taking deposits for those houses, but they don't own any property and they're based in another country so it wouldn't be easy to trace or prosecute them and it's doubtful anyone would get their deposit back."

Gia was thoughtful as she left Mr. Alderton's office. Wanting some peace and quiet, Gia crossed the street to Truro Cathedral.

She prayed for peace for the community of Glasten, prayed for peace for her friend Susan who was in such torment, and prayed for peace in her own household. Above all she asked God to show her how to be content with the changes going on around her. After she felt she was sufficiently prepared, she left the quiet of the church and went to visit her mother.

Gia found her father sitting by a fish pond in the garden. It wasn't much bigger than a bath tub, but installing the pond was the only battle he had won since moving into the house. She pulled up a wicker chair and both of them watched the three koi swim between the water lilies her dad had put in pots and submerged in the shallow pool.

"I will miss this when we move to the retirement community," said her dad. "I didn't realize how much I liked it here."

Following his gaze over the low fence to the hills where in the distance sheep were grazing, Gia had to agree with him. It was a peaceful spot. Both she and her dad were more impressed with feats of nature than those of man.

"I was just in Truro," said Gia wondering whether to wait for her mother before she told her dad what Mr. Alderton had said. "He's been looking into the trust and trying to find a way to stop the tenants from being evicted from Glasten."

"You know your mother's not very pleased that you're involved, don't you. She thinks you're trying to stop us from moving."

"Well, that's just it, Dad. The retirement community has nothing to do with the estate."

"But it's the same land."

"I know that's on the map, but the truth is the college doesn't own the land so how can they sell it to Sandy Dunes or anywhere else? It sounds very fishy to me that people are asked to give them deposits for houses that may never be built."

"They have a limited number of houses. We had to get in quick if we wanted one."

"You didn't already give them a deposit?" Gia asked.

"Your mum . . ."

But as he paused, the French door was flung open.

"Are you causing trouble again, young lady?" asked her mother with a glare that was unmistakable.

Gia was positive that at that very moment, she was her mother's least favorite person.

"It's about the retirement community, love," said her father.

"You just hate us moving to somewhere better than this," her mother spat the words as if they lived in a hovel.

"There is no retirement community," said Gia. "If you want to go on thinking there is, then go right ahead."

Gia's mother's mouth was opening and closing like a guppy, but Gia didn't stop to let her talk.

"I'm trying to protect you," she continued. She was so angry her words came out more of a squeak and her eyes watered. "You stupid woman, why don't you see that not everyone is trying to ruin your perfect little world. There *is* no retirement village. There is no private golf course. It's a scam."

"Now, love. Don't speak to your mum like that," said her dad, but his voice was barely a whisper.

"Call Mr. Alderton. He'll tell you. You remember him, he was the one who did your contract for this *awful* house."

Gia waved her hand in the arc of a rainbow encompassing, the neat little house where she had thought her mum and dad were sure to be happy, but only one of them was.

"And think about him, once in a while." Gia thrust her arm in the direction of her dad. "He loves to sit out here, and watch the sheep in the fields, the birds flying above and the fish swimming in the pond. For once think of him. He's your husband for heaven's sake."

With that, Gia grabbed the French door and considered slamming it. Instead she closed it slowly and through the glass she could see her dad return his gaze to the hills, her mother looked in the pond as if noticing it for the first time.

By the front gate was something that hadn't been there when Gia had arrived at her parent's house – a for sale sign.

Gia drove on down the hill and past Lowenna Antiques and was surprised to see the light on.

"I thought we agreed to close today," said Gia.

"We need to keep those little hands busy and I've told everyone to pop in," said Rose.

And people had indeed popped in. Susan sat at the table with knitted squares in front of her. Mrs. Jones sat across from her and the two of them discussed exactly when Lowenna had been formed. Mrs. Jones thought it was when a saint landed on the shores in the seventh century. Susan wasn't so sure, but her face had a glow Gia hadn't seen for days.

"Wonders never cease," whispered Rose. "Who'd have thought Mrs. Jones would be the one to cheer up Susan."

Iris Trewellyn brought a basket of fresh cakes from the bakery and another lady from the knitting circle placed a tray with tea pot and cups and saucers in front of them.

"Don't forget the sugar," said Susan. "Mrs. Jones does like her two teaspoons of sugar."

When a voluptuous lady leaned over to take a cake, her cleavage was dangerously close to leaving her dress. Rose thrust a safety pin in front of her.

"Do keep those girls in place," Rose said. "You can go in the storage room and sort yourself out."

The woman took the pin, looked down at her heaving bosom and shrugged.

"You're right," said Rose even though the woman hadn't uttered a word. "Take three."

And Rose pushed her in the direction of the storage room.

"What we need," said Gia. "Is an outing. I propose the knitting circle take a mystery tour."

"That would be lovely," said Susan. "Where to?"

"It's a mystery," said Rose her voice sharper than she'd intended. "That's the whole idea," she said a little more softly. "It will be a surprise."

"Oh," Susan continued sorting the squares in front of her in piles of similar colors for Rose to put together.

"Mystery tour?" asked the lady whose dress was now ruched across her décolletage.

"The coaches do tours in the summer. On Fridays it's a mystery. You go somewhere and then have lunch. It's usually a nice ride. We went to those Japanese Gardens one year. Remember that Susan?"

"Susan nodded. Cornwall is the garden capital of the world."

"We need to start doing that again," said Rose.

"We haven't been since you got married," said Susan to Rose.

It was then that Gia realized Susan and Rose's friendship had suffered with Rose's marriage as hers and Holly's had. She'd call Holly and see if she wanted to go on the mystery tour with them. And then she'd make a point of planning things for them to do together. All she'd done lately is stop at the pub and complain about her life, but wasn't her life just wonderful. Look at all these people who were her friends. She glanced around the tiny shop where everyone was gathered. Some were standing, some sitting and each of them there to support their friend, Susan.

Susan would get over this and then she'd be on to the next adventure, but for now her friends were rallying around and looking at the gifts on the table, each of them knew what was important to Susan.

On the table were flowers, chocolates, and an unwrapped plaque with tissue paper beneath and pink ribbon strewn across it.

I am with you; be not dismayed, for I am your God; I will strengthen you, I will help - Isaiah 41:10

That evening Beryl had rounded up all the tenants and Mrs. Gillard on the green centered in Glasten. She gave Gia the pages of the petition. The number of names had grown considerably since Meg's death.

She told them what Mr. Alderton mentioned.

"What does this mean to us?" asked one man.

"Well, it seems complicated, but if you want Mr. Alderton to, he will present your cause to the court."

"I don't know how they can build on this land anyway, even if they bought it," said the man. "We can't. None of the tenants can."

"It *would* cost a lot of money," said Gia, thinking that none of the villagers had finances to build, including Mrs. Gillard.

"Money doesn't come into it," he said. "It's an AONB."

Gia frowned, she couldn't understand what he was saying.

"Area of Natural Beauty," he said. "The same as a national park. You can't build anywhere in Glasten."

"I'll let Mr. Alderton know," said Gia. "He may want to bring that up when he presents your case to the judge."

Chapter 16

Leaving David to work out race strategies with his friends, Gia met Rose and Susan at Lowenna Antiques where they placed a *Closed* sign in the window.

When they reached the coach, she was surprised to see Ruth Rundle arrive with Mrs. Jones. She could only guess that Mrs. Rundle had a tidbit of information that Mrs. Jones wanted to find out and so she would be cozying up to her for the day. But her biggest surprise was her mum.

"I saw her yesterday and told her we were going on a mystery tour today. Felicity said she wanted to come," Rose said almost apologetically.

"I wonder where we're going?" asked Susan as she pressed her nose on the window like a child expecting snow on Christmas morning.

Gia sat alone and was glad of the time to accumulate her thoughts. She took out the cards she'd been working on, each with a suspect in Meg's death.

But it wasn't long before the seat next to her was occupied by her mother. She carried a walking stick patterned like the chintz teapots in their shop.

"Something wrong with your leg, mum?" Gia asked.

"Of course not. All the ramblers use these. I thought it was quaint."

So much for a pleasant day. She wasn't sure which she disliked most – when her mother was happy or when her mother was discontent. Either was grating on her nerves.

"What's dad doing today?" Gia asked.

"I left him sitting in the garden, just staring at those fields. What he's looking at I'll never know."

And she probably wouldn't ever share the joy both Gia and her dad had with natural beauty.

"He's meeting John Trewellyn later."

Gia was glad that her dad had befriended John. He was a good man and her dad enjoyed his company. John was struggling with the loss of Percy and hadn't been out fishing since he was rescued.

Gia's mom reached over and tapped Gia's nose with her index figure.

"You need a thicker foundation to cover up all those freckles," said Felicity. "I've told you for years you need to stay out of the sun or use a sun screen."

Her mum had tried to turn her into a lady with clear porcelain skin, but all their Celtic genes had been dumped on Gia and she had freckles and red hair to prove it. Besides, she'd been very much of a tomboy growing up and her parents more often than not found her up a tree and playing with the boys, rather than discussing new party dresses with the girls.

The deep rumble of the coach's engine burst into life and they were off.

Views from the window were of St. Michael's Mount, the island that revealed a causeway at low tide, but was cut off from the mainland when the sea rushed in.

"Wouldn't it be awful living out there and being cut off from everyone?" asked her mother.

She meant, of course, being cut off from people like those at the golf club. She was sure that if the golf club were an island and her mother was cut off from common folk, she would be perfectly happy, or at least as happy as her mother ever could be.

"Looks like we're going north," said the woman seated behind them.

Gia, who sat by the window, turned and watched the fields, the sheep grazing, a view of the sea and thought how much her dad would have enjoyed the scenery.

"It's colder the farther north you go," observed her mother.

"I doubt we will be driving for more than an hour, probably not a large dip in the temperature, especially in the summer months," said Gia.

Felicity took out her compact, refreshing her makeup and then touched up her lipstick.

"Enjoy the journey, mum," said Gia.

"Rose," said Felicity and leaned over the seat to tap Rose on the shoulder. "Do you know where we're going?"

"It's a surprise," said Susan.

"I don't like surprises," said Felicity quietly.

"What do you like?" asked Gia, but she didn't turn from the window.

Felicity either chose to ignore her or didn't hear.

"That young French man gave us our deposit back," said Felicity. "They're looking into buying in Falmouth now, but I told him I didn't want to move away from my friends."

"Friends?" asked Gia wondering if her mother was talking about the women she drank cocktails with at the golf club bar.

"And of course you. I told him I couldn't move away from my daughter."

Gia doubted that she was included in the conversation. Falmouth was only a few miles away and for a woman who was quite happy to have the Atlantic Ocean between her and her daughter it wouldn't be a deterrent.

"I bet it's the Victorian Gardens," said Susan.

Before her mother could comment, Gia held up her hand.

"Just enjoy the day, mum. Inhale the fresh air, have a nice walk around the gardens, if that's where we're going, and make some new friends."

Behind them, two women were singing and Felicity rolled her eyes.

"Let Ruth get off first," suggested Rose. "She's got that walker to contend with."

And it was Gia's turn to roll her eyes as she watched Ruth struggle down the aisle and then the coach driver assisted her down the steps and then helped her to a bench where she sat and waited for the others.

Rose, Susan, Felicity and Gia followed the pathways and came across a pond covered in lily pads with pink flowers spurting from them. In the center was a small island with Greek columns. Here and there stone moss-covered cherubs stood on pedestals.

"Felicity has a pond," said Rose to Susan.

"Hardly like this," said Felicity.

"But your garden is lovely," said Rose.

"Dad loves it," was all Gia said.

The three ladies left to find the café while Gia sat on the edge of the pond watching a frog hop on lily pads. Behind her was a hedge of rhododendrons and she heard the leaves rustle, and when she turned, Ruth was standing there. She pushed the walker to the side and sat next to Gia.

"No use pretending," Ruth said. "You know don't you," she spat out the words as if accusing Gia. "You know there's nothing wrong with me?"

"But why pretend?" Gia wanted to know.

"For the money. I wasn't well for a while, but when I started recovering I didn't want to lose all the benefits that I was getting."

"And Meg found out?" asked Gia.

Ruth stood.

"Why she couldn't mind her own business I don't know. But she threatened to tell that reporter. Trying to get herself noticed so that she could get him to help her with saving Glasten."

"How did you get her down the stairs?" asked Gia. "Even someone fit would have difficulty getting a dead weight down those narrow stairs. Or did you use the trap door?"

But as she said it, Gia knew that wouldn't have been the case because there were no bruises on Meg other than the head injury.

"She walked. It was an accident. She fell and hit her head. Silly woman thought I was taking her to hospital," said Ruth. "But I got to the car park and shoved her out. She'd lost a lot of blood by then and I didn't think she'd last the night. I thought it was a way to get rid of the little problem."

The little problem as Ruth put it was that Meg had found out about Ruth taking money that she wasn't entitled to.

"She'd been going around upsetting a lot of people. I thought there'd been plenty of suspects."

Gia looked down at the pond, it was deeper than she had first thought and she didn't notice behind her that Ruth had raised her walker and was about to bring it down on Gia.

She had no time to react.

There was nowhere she could move to. Ruth had her pathway blocked.

Gia's breaths became shallow. So she would end up drowning after all. Dying among the tangled in the roots of the lily pads. This was why she'd always had a fear of water.

Gia held up her hands and tried to grab the walker, when she heard the sound of what she could only describe as a jungle cry.

Behind Ruth Gia saw a chintz patterned walking stick and her mother was bringing it down repeatedly on Ruth who let go of the walker.

Gia had continued to hold on and now it was released, she fell back.

Phillip Hodges grabbed her before she hit the water.

"Get her off me," shouted Ruth.

"Call the police," said Phillip and threw his phone to Gia and then twisted Ruth's arm behind her back with one hand and took the cane from Felicity with the other.

"What are you doing here?" asked Gia when Ruth had been taken away, leaving behind her walker that she no longer needed for the charade.

Phillip Hodges shrugged. "I'm a reporter. I thought there was a story. I've been following Ruth Rundle for a while."

"Meg was going to send you a letter, letting you know her suspicions," said Gia.

"She did, but I didn't have anything concrete to go on. I was trying to record your conversation with Ruth." He pocketed his phone. "That was until that woman rushed out of the bushes."

"That woman is my mother," said Gia.

"Oh," said the reporter, returning the cane to Felicity.

"Yes. That's my mother all right," she said with a hint of pride.

"Do you want a lift back?" asked Phillip. "You'll have to file a report at the police station. We all will."

"Can we stop and get me a gin and tonic?" asked Felicity who was wielding the cane like a band leader's baton.

"I'm sure we can," said Phillip.

They were now walking along the pathway and toward the coach where Susan and Rose were waiting.

"We're going back with Phillip," said Gia.

"I think Susan wants to stay with the coach group," said Rose with a sigh.

And they all watched Susan who was standing next to the coach driver who looked like Friar Tuck. Susan smiled and her cheeks glowed.

"I predict we'll be taking lots of coach trips in the future," said Rose. "Here we go again."

Chapter 17

The sun was shining with a slight breeze when nearly three hundred men and women dressed in black wet suits plunged into the sea for a one kilometer swim in the four foot surf. They looked like a pod of seals. For a moment, Gia couldn't spot David until she saw the luminous orange cap bob beneath the wave. She cheered him on, but lost sight again. Swimming in the sea was difficult at the best of times, but packed together like a box of crayons, she had no idea how they could even stay afloat.

Next would be the nearly forty kilometer cycle part of the race, up the hill and on to Goonbell and then Chiverton. The highest part of the race would be the steep run toward the sand dunes finishing not far from Lowenna Antiques and in front of the King William.

It would be at least two hours or more when the first of the entrants would appear and once she saw that David had safely completed the swimming part, she headed to the pub and picked a bench with a view of the green. Holly joined her.

"How's David doing?" she asked when she placed a drink of orange juice and club soda in front of Gia.

"It's hard to tell. I didn't realize there would be so many people. I told him I'd meet him here."

"Good idea," said Holly. "It's better to let him get his focus away from the race before you talk to him. I can't imagine pushing your body like those folks do and this is one of the toughest to complete with all the hills. They come from all over the country. Are you going away tomorrow?"

"I'm wondering if David will still want to. Surely he'll be exhausted. I didn't realize this would be quite so grueling. I've never taken much notice each year when they've had the triathlon here. I've stayed out of the way because it's so crowded. Sitting and drinking coffee and watching them plunge into the sea from my cottage window was close enough for me.

"I heard that you got everything sorted out in Glasten," said Holly.

"Once we found out that it was an AONB, Mr. Alderton said it won't be any problem getting the trust reverted to the original will and Mrs. Gillard will decide who to have as a trustee."

"She doesn't want to take care of it?" asked Holly and sat next to her friend, watching the crowd disperse from the car park.

"She's tired of it all. She wants to move in with her cousin, but she also wants to make sure her husband's wishes are taken care of."

"What will happen to the manor?"

"She can rent it out under the trust." Gia sipped the orange juice and twirled her glass.

"I've got something for you," said Holly and handed Gia a box wrapped in yellow paper. "Don't open it until you get to the hotel."

Gia shook it.

"Just put it in your case," said Holly. "Don't open it, yet."

"Okay, I promise," said Gia.

On Sunday, Gia drove toward Tintagel. David, who was still tired after the race, snoozed in the passenger seat, but she didn't care. She had him all to herself for two whole days. It was better that she drove anyway as her tummy was still a bit queasy.

He'd come in around fifty, which he seemed happy with and Gia had hoped they could put this triathlon behind them and suggested he join the darts team again. David had laughed and said he wanted, with three of his friends, to shatter the hundred year old record for crossing the Atlantic from Lowenna to New York – forty-four days at sea. She laughed with him at the absurdity of four men rowing in a small craft for a month and a half across the ocean.

Gia had booked a massage for David at the hotel spa and walked along the cliffs alone, imagining knights and ladies in long dresses wandering those same cliffs during King Arthur's day. People wandered around the ruins down below and a few brave souls followed a winding stair case down to Merlin's cave.

Returning to the hotel, Gia found the present Holly had given her. She had just opened it when David walked in.

"What's this?" he asked.

"Holly gave it to me. Her little idea of a joke." She dropped the pregnancy test on the bed and slumped her shoulders.

"Try it anyway?" said David. "What's the harm?"

"You don't understand. I can't go through another disappointment."

"But you haven't been feeling well."

"It was just a virus. Susan had it too and we know she's not pregnant."

They both looked at each other, neither breaking the stare.

"Okay. I'll do it. But I don't want to hear any more about it after you realize it's negative. We agreed to wait until next year."

But it wasn't negative.

When the second line became a solid pink and made a plus sign, Gia sat on the stool in the bathroom and her heart plunged.

This had been what she wanted. This had been what they both wanted. She had only asked that they wait because she didn't want to face any more failures.

But would this push them apart again?

Would David be off running and making new friends while she was at home with a baby?

"Gia?" David called. "Are you all right?"

She took a deep breath and opened the door. She cleared her throat and spoke quietly.

"Do you still like the name Rowena?" she asked.

David bit his lip and held out his arms to her. From the corner of his eye, Gia could swear she saw a tear.

THE END

Author Notes

When I first moved to Texas I was shopping in Sears department store and the sales clerk asked where I was from. When I told her I had moved from England, she sighed and said she had travelled extensively, but not to other countries because she was concerned with not knowing other languages. She then asked what language they spoke in England. I looked at her for what seemed a full minute, trying to judge if she was joking. She wasn't.

But English, whether written or spoken, can be different, which became even more evident when I started writing my first novel, A Graceful Death.

As the Lowenna series is based in Cornwall, I wrote it with all the English phrases using words like car park instead of parking lot, windscreen wipers instead of windshield, lorry instead of truck, torch instead of flashlight, serviette instead of napkin, boot instead of trunk – you get the picture. It was when I began to read in front of a critique group that I realized many of the English words and phrases were completely baffling the listeners. I decided to write for an American audience and what resulted was a mixture of English and American English. Hopefully, my English readers won't be too critical and my American readers will be able to read the story without stopping to try and understand what a bin man (trash collector) or bonnet (car hood) is. Any uncommon words to the American ear that I used, I described or elaborated upon. The word grey was replaced with gray (except Earl Grey tea).

Then there's the punctuation. Again, I used American punctuation. What's the difference you may ask? In England single quote marks are used and the full stop (period) comes after the quote mark.

And the young sales girl? After explaining they spoke English in England, she then divulged all the places she had travelled to: East Texas, West Texas and South Texas. Where, apparently, they all spoke English.

Acknowledgments

I have many people to thank for making my novels possible. Encouragement from my family – My son, Nathan. My daughter, Cheryl and son-in-law Jeff and the new additions, Perryn, Kate and Vaughn, my precious grandchildren, who are sure to show up as characters in later novels.

I must also thank many friends who often find they have unknowingly contributed to the dialog.

Members of Trinity Writers' Workshop have, over the years, offered invaluable critique and encouragement and become dear friends.

ALSO BY ANN SUMMERVILLE

A Graceful Death
(No. 1 in the Lowenna Series)

Giovanna Matthews has an acceptable life in London with her own flat, a good job, and recent engagement to the son of a Scottish landowner. But not long after her engagement to Alan, news of Aunt Grace's death hits her like a red double decker bus. Ignoring his pleas to stay, she bundles her dog and suitcase into a rusty Volkswagen and drives to her aunt's cottage on the Cornish coast. Although her intent is to take care of Aunt Grace's affairs and leave the village quickly, she is persuaded to join the local knitting circle and rekindles old friendships. Further complicating her decision to leave Lowenna is her attraction to David, a childhood friend. Although the villagers are closed mouthed about her aunt's demise it soon becomes clear to Giovanna that not only is her aunt's death no accident but there is a family secret involving her missing cousin.

High Tide
(No. 2 in the Lowenna Series)

Giovanna Matthews settles happily into the English west country village of Lowenna, but a storm is about to rock her world. Distressing the ladies from the knitting circle, a body drifts in with a high tide. Unconvinced the death is an accident, Gia leaves no pebble unturned while sleuthing her way around the village. Her delving further disrupts village life much to the distress of many villagers who want every rock to stay firmly in place. Meanwhile, her boyfriend, David, has an unwelcome visitor who threatens to unravel the bonds that tie him and Gia. Can Gia solve the mystery and encourage the visitor to leave before her anchor in the village is uprooted and she too is cast out to sea?

Gwinnel Gardens
(No. 3 in the Lowenna Series)

It wasn't unusual for retirees in Lowenna to succumb to death
during the winter months in Lowenna, but while Gia and her
friend, Holly worked on restoring the overgrown Gwinnel
Gardens, they noticed that there were an increasing number of
services at the crematorium in the valley. After hearing the
President of Gwinnel Gardens had died unexpectedly, Gia dug
in her heels and decided to investigate. After all this was a great
way to avoid plans for her upcoming wedding which everyone
seemed to have an idea of what she should wear. But unless she
found out quickly who was behind the sudden deaths, would
someone close to Gia be the next victim?

Storms & Secrets

In search of her husband, Heather reluctantly travels from London to his Texas home town where she is vocal about her dislike of snakes, spiders, and cowboys. She vows to spend no more than two weeks away from her city apartment but finds a slew of secrets swirling like a Texas tornado. While her husband keeps his emotional distance, and she tries to maintain her British reserve, Heather is nevertheless intrigued by the friendliness of Fort Worth locals. Despite developing friendships, Heather struggles to find out what illness her mother-in-law is suffering from, how a neighbor fits into her husband's past and why a vagrant sits across the street each day staring at the house. One by one, Heather uncovers the mysteries surrounding her husband's family. Can her marriage be saved, and will her new Texas friends entice Heather to share their love for the Lone Star State?

The Berton Hotel

At the end of the millennium, Lily found herself driving toward a small Texas town where her great grandmother had disappeared over fifty years ago. Expecting to escape from yet another relationship in California that hadn't ended well, the first person she meets is a charming Texan with brown eyes and blond hair. While trying to avoid anything that might resemble a romantic encounter, Lily gets to know the citizens of Crystal Wells and uncovers a lot more than her great grandmother's disappearance in 1935. A mystery buried deeper than one of the local wells may bring to light more secrets than Lily has bargained for.

Grandmother's Flower Garden
(No. 1 in the Pecan Valley series)

When Bea first arrives in Pecan Valley she's accompanied by thunder and lightning, and she tells herself the storm will pass. She also tries to convince herself that she's taking an early retirement, looking for a quiet place to work on her quilts, putter around in her new garden. But returning to the place where the event happened thirty years ago sparks a longing to find out what took place after Bea left Pecan Valley. Although the clouds have now dissipated, another storm is hovering over her new home and when someone is murdered, she has second thoughts about moving to a small Texas town.

Ann Summerville was born in England, and in search of a warmer climate, moved to California before settling in Texas. Her short stories and flash fiction have been published in Chicken Soup for the Soul, The Lutheran Digest, Long Story Short, The Shine Journal, Doorknobs & Bodypaint, Associated Content, Trinity Writer's Workshop newsletters and also their collection of Christmas stories. A member of Trinity Writer's Workshop, Ann is currently working on another cozy mystery. Ann resides in Fort Worth with her son, two boisterous dogs and a somewhat elusive cat.

www.annsummerville.com

www.cozyintexas.blogspot.com

Made in the USA
Lexington, KY
24 February 2013